DES HUNT
SUNKEN FOREST

First published in 2016 by Scholastic New Zealand Limited
Private Bag 94407, Botany, Auckland 2163, New Zealand

Scholastic Australia Pty Limited
PO Box 579, Gosford, NSW 2250, Australia

Sunken Forest © Des Hunt, 2016

ISBN 978-1-77543-403-0

National Library of New Zealand Cataloguing-in-Publication Data

Hunt, Des, 1941-
Sunken forest / Des Hunt.
ISBN 978-1-77543-403-0
[1. School camps—Fiction. 2. Children of prisoners—Fiction.
3. Interpersonal conflict—Fiction.] I. Title.
NZ823.3—dc 23

12 11 10 9 8 7 6 5 4 3   7 8 9 / 1

Photography Credits: Front cover background image © Cristian Dimitrius; eel © Can ·
Stock Photo Inc./lucidwaters.
Back cover image: © Vida and Luke Kelly Design.

Publishing team: Lynette Evans, Penny Scown, and Sophia Broom
Design: Smartwork Creative, www.smartworkcreative.co.nz
Typeset in Flux 11.5pt
Printed in Australia by Griffin Press

Scholastic New Zealand's policy is to use papers that are renewable and made efficiently from wood grown in sustainable forests, so as to minimise its environmental footprint.

DES HUNT
SUNKEN FOREST

SCHOLASTIC
AUCKLAND SYDNEY NEW YORK LONDON TORONTO
MEXICO CITY NEW DELHI HONG KONG

CONTENTS

Prologue...7

~~~~~~~~~~~~~~~~~~~~ **PART ONE** ~~~~~~~~~~~~~~~~~~~~

One Good Turn 13
Cam and Jay... 18
Attacked 26
Accusations 34
Punishment...43

~~~~~~~~~~~~~~~~~~~~ **PART TWO** ~~~~~~~~~~~~~~~~~~~~

Azura..53
The Sunken Forest 62
Galley Slave... 72
Monstrous Eel...80
Earthquakes and Landslides................................88
Onepoto Caves 93
The Search 101
Alone 113
Revenge...122

Munn 130

Burma Trail 140

Taniwha 150

Wasps..159

Missing Meat..168

Rain...178

Morning..184

Disaster 192

Failure...199

Lost..207

Aftermath 215

Watch 224

PART THREE

Hero...233

Villain..241

Detective Smith...249

Assembly...258

Epilogue 267

PROLOGUE

With every trail of connected events there may be many starting points. Mostly this is because those involved have a different view of where and how it began. And so it is with the events recorded in this story.

For Police Inspector Lewis Armstrong, the trail started sixty years ago and involved his father Graham. In January of 1957, Graham was staying at Lake Waikaremoana with a group of other boys. On a beautiful Wednesday morning they all went for a swim in the lake. After getting in the water, Graham remembered he was wearing his watch, a gift from his parents for his fifteenth birthday just a few weeks before. Not wanting to damage the new watch, he took it off, reached up and placed it on a grassy bank. After that, he forgot about it until the following morning. When he returned, the only sign of anything ever being on the grass was a pile of swan poo. The watch had gone.

Over the next sixty years, first Graham and then his son, Lewis, would return to the lake, always hopeful that some miracle event would reveal the watch. However, when that event did finally occur, there was no time to rejoice, for it came with a disaster that affected the lives of everyone involved.

Elsa, another participant, would tell the story differently – if she could talk, that is. The starting point for Elsa would be in 1917 when an old Maori man sat beside a river scooping up baby eels, each no longer than his little finger. He called them ngaeroero, preferring the Tuhoe name to the English 'elvers'. Soon afterwards, with hundreds of the tiny fish swimming around in a glass jar, he mounted his horse and rode up a trail that would take him high into the mountains above the river. Half a day later he reached his destination and looked out over the lake known as Waikaremoana, its waters edged with grey cliffs and backed by hills stretching, layer after layer, until clouds and land became one.

At the lake's edge, he immersed the jar and watched as the ngaeroero found their way out into the green water. When all had gone, he stood, gazed over the lake and spoke for some time, asking the lake to nurture the eels, so that one day they would provide kai for his mokopuna – his grandchildren. As it turned out, one of those eels eluded his mokopuna – and even their mokopuna– to end up as the biggest longfin eel ever seen. An eel that had an important role in the events that followed.

The main person in this story, however, is Matthew Smith, known as Matt. He would say the story began when he was sent to live with his nana in Gisborne — or 'Gizzy' as many New Zealanders call it. Up until then he'd lived with his two sisters and brother at their home in Hastings, but then his dad, Brayden, lost his job, making money pretty tight. Being the eldest — he was eleven at the time — Matt was the one who had to be sent away.

Actually, it was more complicated than that. Brayden lost his job because he was sent to prison for reckless driving. This was not the first time he'd been charged, but it was his first time in prison. He was a panelbeater, and cars were his passion. Many would call him a boy racer.

While it was the actions of his father that brought Matt into this story, it was the reaction of others that took him to the lake and everything that came afterwards.

PART ONE

1

ONE GOOD TURN

This all started on a Tuesday morning in February, Matt Smith's fourth week at Gisborne's Oneroa Intermediate School. He was walking to school, with his bag on his back containing the lunch Nana had made and a book he was meant to be reading … but in two weeks he hadn't got past page five. It was rubbish-collection day, and the footpath was lined with recycling bins and plastic bags. There was plenty of room for them as the street was one of those with a wide footpath and old houses set back from the road. It was while passing one of these that he heard a faint voice.

"Young man," came the croaky call. "Can you help me?" There was pleading in the tone but no urgency. "Please?"

Looking up he saw an old woman halfway along a grassy drive.

"Young man," she called again. "I need some help with my recycling bin. I can't handle it by myself."

Although he was already running late for school, Matt said, "Yeah, okay."

That was the deciding moment, which is probably the real beginning of these events. For if he'd said, "Nah, I've gotta get to school," he would never have gone to the lake and played no part in all that followed.

Of course, as he walked down the drive, he knew nothing of this. He was simply going to help an old lady take out the rubbish. And she really was an old lady. He thought Nana was old at fifty-six, but he could see that this woman was truly ancient: body bowed, pure white hair, and wrinkles so deep that the skin would have needed pulling apart to wash down in the valleys. She didn't move too well either, which was why she needed help: she could hardly move herself, let alone an overflowing recycling bin.

"I haven't put it out for months," she explained as she led him around the back. "It's too hard."

The bin was mostly full of empty food cans: spaghetti, baked beans, peaches, pears … There were a few drink bottles; no alcohol ones though. And while it wasn't heavy, it was awkward to carry, being filled far too high.

Together they staggered down the drive, Matt stopping every few steps to pick up a fallen can and the woman dragging a near-empty black bag sealed with a blue sticker. When both containers had been aligned with the neighbours',

Matt said goodbye and took a few steps towards school.

"Taihoa!" she said. "I must reward you in some way."

Reward! What kid can ignore that word? Certainly not Matt, and that led to a second decision that could have been different. He followed her down the drive and into her house.

The living area was incredibly neat. Nothing, absolutely nothing was in the wrong place. Except for Matt. The room was so different to anything he'd been in before that he stood half in the doorway, unsure of whether to go any further.

"Come in. Come in," she urged. "Don't be frightened."

But still he felt nervous taking a couple of steps forward. That was when he found that everything *wasn't* quite perfect; there was a strong smell of cigarette smoke. Someone in the house was a smoker.

"That's better," she said, moving to a set of cupboards against the wall. Five photos were arranged neatly on the top: a group photo in the middle, with individual portraits to the side — three men and a woman.

She adjusted one, which to her eyes wasn't quite in the right place. "My family," she said.

Matt mentally braced himself to be introduced to each in turn. Instead, she crouched, opened a cupboard and reached inside with both hands. When upright again, she was holding a large object that she slid, with some difficulty, into the clear space in front of the group photo.

It was a very large cookie jar. Matt's jaw dropped, not only because of the size of the jar, but because of the contents. Not cookies — money! It was full of money. More money than Matt had ever seen in one place before.

At the bottom were coins, mostly gold ones. Above them were the notes: five- and ten-dollar notes, pushed in so tightly that it would have been impossible to dig down to the coins without notes spilling everywhere.

"My small-change jar," said the old woman. "It's getting a bit full these days. I don't seem to have as much need for money as I once did."

Small change! he thought. *Our family could live on that for weeks.*

"How much would you like?" she asked, fishing into the jar and pulling out a handful.

"Um … ah …"

Matt had a problem: from the time he was little, his parents had told him never to take money from strangers. "They'll always want something in return," his dad would say. "And it will be something that is not nice."

Although he couldn't imagine this woman wanting something 'not nice' from him, accepting her money would have been the same as peeing on her floor. It was one of the no-no's his parents had programmed into his brain for the previous eleven years. So a third decision was made.

"No, I can't take your money," he said quietly.

For a time she simply looked at him. Then she smiled,

nodding her head slowly as if that was the right answer. "Then how about a scone with strawberry jam? Freshly baked this morning because I've got the plumber coming later and he always likes my scones."

Still Matt hesitated, knowing that school must have already started.

Her eyes twinkled. "I promise they're not poisoned."

"All right," said Matt, and by uttering those two words, Matthew Smith took that third step which toppled him past the point of no return.

2

CAM AND JAY

The taste of strawberry jam was still in Matt's mouth when he walked into the school office to sign-in. Opening the Late-comers' Book, he wrote:

Matthew Smith 4SG 9.35am
Helping old lady put out rubbish

He then went to Room 4 where Mrs Snodgrass was at the whiteboard teaching English. She pulled an annoyed face when Matt opened the door, before pointing to his desk. When he was seated, she continued with the lesson.

There was nothing special about Mrs Snodgrass except for her name – which wasn't really hers as she took it from her husband when she got married. She'd been Matt's teacher for only four weeks and already he'd heard seven different variations, ranging from Snotgrass to combinations that were more like swear words, although nobody used any of them to her face.

She was an okay teacher, but Matt wasn't a great fan of her sort of schoolwork: English and social studies were not his thing. Maths was all right, as was PE. Science and technology were his favourites. If he'd had either of those first period he would never have been late for school. But they had those in the afternoon and with specialist teachers.

His other favourite subjects were interval, lunchtime and end-of-school. In Hastings he'd been good at those subjects because he'd had lots of friends, but at Oneroa Intermediate he wasn't doing so well. The kids in his class were friendly enough, but didn't go out of their way to include him in their games. In the whole of the school, only two boys had welcomed him into their group: Cameron Nelson and Jayden Cross.

After the bell went for interval, Matt found Cam and Jay in their usual place: down the back of the grounds by the caretaker's shed. Cameron was the bigger of the two and clearly the dominant one. He sneered rather than smiled, he intentionally wore his uniform in disarray and regularly disobeyed school rules. His trademark was an against-the-rules silvery chain worn around his neck. Although Matt had known him only a short time, he'd already noticed that duty staff avoided Cameron Nelson, knowing that contact was sure to lead to an argument.

Jay was smaller, quieter and better dressed. He seemed prepared to tag along with whatever the bigger boy had in mind. Of the two, Matt liked Jay better.

"You late this morning?" asked Cam as Matt sat down.

"Yeah."

"We were looking for you. You got your bag at school?"

Matt nodded. "Why?"

"Where is it?"

"Hanging in the porch outside my room."

"You shouldn't leave it there," said Cam. "People steal stuff."

"Nothing in it worth stealing."

"Someday there will be," said Jay. He pointed to their two bags resting against the fence. "You should carry it with you like we do. That way you'll never lose anything."

"Go and get it now," said Cameron. It was an order, not a request.

Reluctantly, Matt stood and wandered back to the classroom. Unfortunately, Mrs Snodgrass was returning at the same time. She saw Matt and insisted that he go inside and do the work he'd missed due to lateness. That took the rest of interval and Matt never got back to his friends with the bag.

All that week, the period between interval and lunch was set down for class camp preparation. On the coming Monday they were off to Auckland for their week-long Big City Camp. Preparation was mostly bookwork and research about the places they'd be visiting. The zoo, a theme park and a train ride seemed like they'd be fun, but Matt wasn't all that excited about going to see a play. Mostly, he was looking forward to the experience, with just a little apprehension about spending a whole week with people he hardly knew.

Matt thought nothing more about schoolbags until last period when he was working on his materials project in the technology room. Looking out the window he saw Jayden and Cameron being marched towards the office by the principal, Mrs Dingle. Both boys had bags on their backs.

Half an hour later the office runner came in with a notice to be read out to the class: *Because of on-going problems, no holographic swap cards are to be brought to school. If any student is found with these cards, they will be confiscated and held until the end of term.*

A groan went up from the class. Not long afterwards they heard the same moaning from the class next door. Clearly the banning of holographic swap cards was not a popular move. Matt couldn't care less. The cards were given out by supermarkets if you spent $50. Each card had a spectacular 3D holographic image from a popular TV series. As Nana never spent $50 at any one time, there were never any cards to collect.

Other kids did though, and groups would gather to swap and even sell cards. Sometimes fights would start over the cards, which was probably why they'd been banned. Matt would find out soon enough that there was also another reason.

Matt's route home from school was the reverse of the one taken in the morning. As usual, he walked alone. The other kids didn't exactly ignore him, they were just too busy chatting to their mates. The few attempts he'd made to join into a group had resulted in questions that he didn't want to answer. As a result, he kept to himself, except for Cam and Jay who seemed to have no interest in his past. But they lived in the opposite direction so he never saw them outside of school — except on that day.

"Matt! Matt! Wait up!"

He turned and saw Jay and Cam running up.

"What's the rush?" Matt asked as they came alongside.

"You!" said Cam.

"You took off so quickly," added Jay.

"Nobody said I had to wait."

"Well, we're telling you now." That was Cam. "Follow us."

They crossed the road and walked along to an empty section almost opposite to where the old lady lived. There were concrete paths leading to and from a bare patch where a house had once stood. Down the back was a mess of overgrown plants. Judging by the rubbish scattered under the bushes they weren't the first to use it as a meeting place.

"Give us your bag," ordered Cam.

"Why?"

"Give it to me. Now!"

Matt slipped his arms out of the straps and handed it over.

Instead of opening the main part, containing his empty lunchbox and book, Cam unzipped the pocket at the front. His hand went in ... and came out with a thick wad of cards. Holographic swap cards.

Immediately Matt understood everything: Cam and Jay had stolen these and he'd been used to get them out of school. They must have put them in there during lunchtime.

"Yeah!" said Jay, watching Cam count the cards. "How many are there?"

They waited for Cam to finish.

"Sixty-eight. Thirty each for you and me, and eight for Matt." He counted off eight cards and held them out. "There you are. That's your share."

"I don't collect them."

Cam looked at Jay, and together they burst out laughing — forced, ridiculing laughter.

"We don't collect them either," said Jay. "We sell them."

Cam nodded. "We can get a dollar a card for the common ones, ten bucks for the rare ones."

"You won't be able to sell them at school," said Matt.

"They've been banned."

More ridiculing laughter. "We don't sell them at *our* school, moron," said Cam. "We hang outside places where the rich kids go. There's always plenty of buyers." He pocketed the cards. "C'mon, let's go. We can sell some of these today."

As they moved out onto the footpath, it so happened that the old lady was on the other footpath picking up the now empty bin. She saw Matt and waved.

"Hello," she shouted in her croaky, weak voice. "Do you want another scone?"

"No, thank you. I've got to get home."

"All right, dear. Maybe next week."

Walking away, Jay turned and asked, "Do you know her?"

"Nah, I just helped her put her bin out this morning. That's why I was late."

Jay thought about that. "And she gave you a scone?" A nod. "She made scones just for you?"

"Nah. She made them for the plumber."

"Which plumber?" asked Cam, showing interest for the first time.

"How would I know?"

"But you've been into her house?"

"Yeah."

"What's she got in there?"

The question surprised Matt and he took some time to

reply. "Nothing much. All I saw was lots of photos."

That wasn't enough for Cam. "Anything valuable?"

Warning sirens started going off in Matt's head. "No!" he said quickly, shaking his head. "No."

Cam's eyes narrowed. "You're a hopeless liar, Matt. What's she got in there?"

Matt shook his head again. "Nothing!"

"All right," said Cam quietly. "We'll see. We'll find out, won't we, Jay?"

3

ATTACKED

"Make any new friends today?"

This was the fifteenth time Nana had asked this question since Matt started at Oneroa Intermediate. Every schoolnight over dinner the question would be asked. And every night, except for one, the answer had been "No." The exception was when he'd told her about hanging out with Cameron Nelson and Jayden Cross.

"It will happen," said Nana, as she always did. "No need to rush it. Early friends aren't always good ones." They ate in silence for a while. "So, did anything else happen at school today?"

This question had also been asked fifteen times. "I helped an old lady put out her recycling bin on the way to school."

"That was good of you. How old? Old like me — or older?"

"Dinosaur old."

"Oh, yeah," said Nana, smiling. "And where does this dinosaur live?"

Matt didn't yet know the names of the streets, so he explained his route to school, identifying the place that way.

Nana's interest picked up. "What does this woman look like?"

"White hair. And really deep wrinkles on her face."

Nana started nodding. "And a croaky voice, I bet."

"Yes! Do you know her?"

"Agnes Williams. She really is ancient. Must be nearly ninety now. I'm amazed she's lived so long — she smokes like a chimney."

"The house stank of cigarettes."

Nana's eyes widened. "You went inside?"

"Yeah. She offered me some money. She had this ginormous cookie jar full of notes and coins."

"I hope you didn't accept any of it." He shook his head. "Good boy. That was the right move, Matt. "

"She gave me a scone instead," he added. "Made a joke about it not being poisoned."

Nana chuckled. "Can't have been, either, seeing as you're still here. Now, if it had been her daughter who'd done the baking, it could've been a different story. I went to school with Sharon. She was bit of a witch then — and still is from what I hear. Doesn't sound like she's looking after her mother too well, either. She should be the one making sure the recycling bin gets put out instead of leaving it to her mum to beg others to do it."

Later, when they were doing the dishes, Nana raised the topic again. "This jar you saw at Mrs Williams, was there a lot of money in it?"

"Heaps and heaps. Hundreds of dollars."

"And she just had it sitting there where anyone could see it?"

"No. She took it out of a cupboard. It was so heavy she could hardly lift it."

"Did she put it away again?"

Matt shrugged. "Dunno. When I left it was still sitting on top of the cupboard."

Nana stopped washing dishes and looked at her grandson. "You haven't told anybody at school about this money, have you?"

"No."

"Good. Don't talk about it to anyone. Some people might start getting nasty thoughts if they hear she's got lots of cash sitting around. An old woman like that is an obvious target. She could so easily get hurt."

Nana Smith always went to bed straight after the dishes. She didn't like watching television much, preferring to read romantic stories in bed. Often she would fall asleep after an hour or so, snoring loudly enough for it to be heard from the lounge.

Matt was different: he liked TV and hated reading. So the arrangement suited him fine as he could watch what he liked. Except that night he couldn't find much, so he surfed channels, not really taking anything in. His mind was elsewhere, back in the old lady's living room. He'd enjoyed his time with her, eating a scone and talking about Gizzy. She knew so much about the place, having lived there all her ninety years.

What concerned him now was that he might have put her in danger. She was so fragile that even the slightest thing would cause injury. Nana was right; she shouldn't leave her money out for people to see. Maybe he could do something about that.

Leaving the lounge he moved to his bedroom, pausing for a moment to listen to the snoring as he passed Nana's room. From his top drawer he removed a school notebook left over from his days in Hastings. Taking his time — his writing was no better than his reading — he wrote a note warning the woman not to leave her money where it could be seen. He thought of signing it but decided against this as he'd never told her his name. Ripping out the page, he grabbed a torch, stuck it in his pocket and quietly let himself out of the house.

A rising full moon combined with a faint glow from the western horizon made the torch unnecessary. At 9:30 in the evening there was still enough traffic about for him not to feel too scared about being out alone. Anyway, who would want to attack him? He owned nothing that others would want.

The traffic had thinned by the time he got to Mrs Williams' street. Although the remains of the sunset had gone, the moon was now higher, giving brighter highlights and darker shadows. A warm wind blew down off the hills.

His original plan had been to leave the note in the letterbox. This changed when he saw that the flap at the back of the letterbox was missing; a piece of paper put in there would be blown away within a minute. Plan B was to put it in the house if he could. Maybe the place was so old that it had a letter flap in the door.

Walking around the house he was pleased to see that every window was shut. Mrs Williams might leave her money lying around, but it looked as though she was aware of the need for security. No one would get in there without making a lot of noise.

There was no flap in the front door, nor the back. However, the back doorstep was so worn, that there was a gap between it and the bottom of the door. Taking out the note, he knelt down on the top step. As he was feeding the paper carefully into the gap, a gust of wind whipped it from his fingers, zipping it away into the house. Where it went from there, Matt could not tell, but at least it was inside, and the way the woman kept the house neat and clean, it was sure to be found in the morning.

Instead of returning down the drive, he went around the other side of the house, planning to take a shortcut across the front of the place next door. Not a good move. Standing on a gravel driveway between the two houses was a giant of a man. Although his back was turned, this was little relief to Matt, for it revealed the red and white gang patch on his leather jacket saying *Gizzy Pits*. Matt turned to sneak back. Unfortunately his foot scraped against the gravel, rattling the stones.

"What the—" growled the man, turning.

Matt took off around the back of the old lady's house. Staying in the shadows, he crept around the walls, not knowing whether the man was in pursuit or not. He was about to make the dash to the road, when a shape moved into the moonlight ahead of him.

Another gangster? Or the same one?

Either way, it was time to hide. Several overgrown bushes were nearby. He chose the thickest and crawled in until he was tight against the trunk. He crouched low, hoping his heavy breathing couldn't be heard outside.

Something must have attracted the man's attention, for soon Matt heard scuffling of feet and grunts as the bushes nearby were searched.

"I know you're in there," growled a voice. "Come out before I have to come in."

Matt shuffled around the trunk away from the sound. He'd wait until the man came in for him and then escape out the other side.

At least that was the plan. Instead, a branch scraping across his face made him cry out. Before he had a chance to run, a large arm stretched through the leaves, grabbed his arm and hauled him out into the moonlight.

There was only one gangster, but one was scary enough for Matt. The man towered over him, his heavily tattooed face making him look more zombie-like than human.

"What you doing round here?"

Matt thought quickly. "Taking a shortcut."

"You don't take shortcuts through our turf."

Matt's whole body was shaking, so it took little extra effort to shake his head.

But that wasn't enough for the man. Still holding him by the arm, he began dragging him around the back of the old lady's house. Only when he was on the gravel drive did he stop. He turned Matt around so that he was looking up the drive.

"See that?" growled the man. "You wanna shortcut? That's your shortcut to hell."

Up the drive behind an open gate was a rough house surrounded by dead vehicles fenced in with high corrugated iron. As he looked, Matt heard multiple chains rattle, followed by several deep growls.

"They're pits," said the gangster. "Pit bulls – and they're hungry. You wanna see them fed?"

More shaking from Matt.

"No? Then don't take shortcuts near here." A pause. "I'm gonna let you go. But next time you get this."

A fist was thrust out at Matt's face, stopping so close that he flinched. A letter was tattooed on each knuckle. Matt had to move his head back to get them into focus.

P-A-I-N spelled the letters. Then the gangster let go of Matt so that he could bring the other fist into view. Now the letters read D-E-E-P P-A-I-N.

"Get the message?"

Matt organised his shaking enough to make it look like a nod.

"Then go!" This was reinforced with a shove from both hands that caused Matt to sprawl onto the gravel.

"Now!"

Matthew Smith went.

4

ACCUSATIONS

As Matt walked to school on Wednesday morning, he paused to study the scene of his encounter the previous night. Everything looked quite peaceful in daylight: the house down the gravel drive beside the old lady's house looked less sinister and the fences not so high. The gate was now closed, blocking out the sound from both the gang and the pit bulls inside.

Behind Mrs Smith's house he could see the tail-end of a van, painted purple and decorated with a maze of white pipes. He could see the beginnings of the word *Plumber*, but no other name. He sniffed the air, wondering if the plumber would get scones two days in a row. There was nothing other than the dusty smells of summer.

Nothing much happened at school that day, except Matt intentionally stayed away from Jayden and Cameron. Although he'd taken steps to protect Mrs Smith's money, he didn't want any more questions about what might be in the house. Anyway he was still angry about being used to carry stolen goods out of the school. The last thing Matt wanted was to get involved in any thieving activity, for he already knew what an impact that could have on his life.

Towards the end of the previous year, soon after his father went to prison, Matt got caught stealing at a shop near school. The shoplifting wasn't planned, he was just looking around this toyshop when he picked up a magnifying glass, thought it would be a great thing to have, and put it in his pocket. After leaving the shop, the owner came after him. He gave the thing back, provided his name and hoped that would be the end of the matter. Except it wasn't; the shop owner had a daughter at Matt's school and told her.

A few days later when a packet of felt-tips went missing in class, Matt was accused of stealing them. From then on, whenever anything was mislaid, somebody would say that Matt had stolen it. Before the shoplifting, everyone called him Matt; afterwards it was always Matthew — Matthew the thief. It was actually a relief to move up to live with Nana.

During camp prep on Thursday, the office lady came to the class to collect Matt and his bag. The principal wanted to see him. Like Cam and Jay had on Tuesday, Matt had to make the long walk across the quad, bag on back, trying to work out what it might be about. Waiting in the reception area, reading a magazine, was a woman who at a glance looked vaguely familiar. But before he could get a decent look, he was ushered into the principal's office.

"Take a seat, Matthew," said Mrs Dingle without taking her eyes from the computer.

Matt knew what would happen next: there would be a period of silence while she pretended to be working and he was meant to start worrying about why he might be there. The situation was familiar from his previous school. This time he studied the surroundings, which he'd not seen before, determined not to let the waiting get to him.

It didn't work. The room had nothing of interest and this principal could play the silence game better than he could. After fifteen minutes he was a mess of worry.

Finally, she wheeled her chair away from the computer to sit behind the desk directly opposite. "Do you know why you're here, Matthew?"

He shook his head.

"You were late to school on Tuesday." This was said as

if it was a major crime.

"I signed the late book."

"I know you did. You gave the reason as ..." From the side of her desk she pulled over the Latecomers' Book. "'Helping old lady put out rubbish.' Would you care to expand on that?"

No, I don't care to, was Matt's first thought, but he knew there was no choice. He explained how the old lady had called out to him and he'd carried the bin to the footpath for her. No mention was made of the reward.

"Is that it?"

"Yes."

"What about being invited into the house for a reward?"

This shook him. "Yeah, well, the lady said she wanted to give me something, so I went inside with her and had a scone."

Her eyebrows rose. "There was no mention of money?"

"Um, yeah, there was. She had a cookie jar full of cash and wanted to give me some. I said no. That's when she offered me a scone."

"Which you did accept, topped with strawberry jam."

Matt stayed perfectly still, knowing that they had reached a critical point.

"Have you been back to the house since then?"

"I walk past it on the way to school and home again."

"You've not been back inside?"

"No!"

The principal let out a long sigh. "The thing is, Matthew, waiting in reception is somebody who says you went back to the house yesterday, you went to the cupboard where that money was stored and you stole it. What have you got to say to that?"

"It's not true. She's lying."

"I don't think she is. She's certainly not lying about the money going missing."

"Well, I didn't take it!"

"Mmm …" A silence followed before she asked, "Did you tell anyone else about the money?"

Matt hesitated. Here was the moment where he could tell her about Cam and Jay's interest. In the end he said, "No."

She shook her head a few times before standing. "All right, I'm going to bring in Ms Williams and see if she can help you remember."

This time Matt recognised her: she was in one of the photos on the old lady's cupboards.

"Ms Williams, this is Matthew Smith."

The woman stared at him. "Did you say 'Smith'?"

"I did. Matthew Smith."

The woman began to nod her head slowly. "Matthew Smith," she repeated. "I bet you're the son of Brayden Matthew Smith."

That was his dad's name but he wasn't admitting anything to this person.

"I went to school with your grandmother," she continued.

"We were good friends once. I watched your Dad grow up. I always knew he'd end up where he is today."

Matt had been trying to keep eye contact, but after this statement he had to look away.

She turned to the principal. "Do you know that his father's in prison?"

That was clearly news to Mrs Dingle.

The woman was nodding again. "Like father, like son, eh Matthew? Both thieves."

"I'm not a thief. Neither is Dad."

"That might not be the reason he's in prison, but he was a thief when he lived in Gisborne. And you are too. I can prove it."

"How?"

She gave him a smirking smile. "The jar, Matthew. I found the jar."

Matt was starting to get mad. "So what? That doesn't prove I took it."

"Oh yes, it does. See, when Mum told me she'd seen the same boy coming out of the empty section across the road, I thought I'd go and take a look. And there was the jar. No money, but it was definitely the same jar. You took that money, emptied it into your schoolbag and left the jar behind."

"When?"

"Sometime yesterday."

"But it was the day before when she saw me come out

39

of the section."

"It's your hiding place. I bet you go there after all your thieving."

"No! I'm not a thief."

"Matthew, come on," said Mrs Dingle, in a disappointed voice. "Who else could it be?"

That's when Matt remembered something. "The scones!" he said. "The old lady said she made the scones because the plumber was coming. See? Other people have been to the house. Someone else could have taken it."

Ms Williams snorted. "Yes, the plumber did come that day, and yesterday as well. But if you're blaming the plumber we've used for more than thirty years, then you're crazy as well as a thief. Anyway, by the time the plumber came, the jar was back in the cupboard."

By then Matt was desperate. "What about the gang that lives near her house? They could have stolen it."

The woman burst out laughing. "The Gizzy Pits? They're so tame, people call them the Gizzy *Pets*. Those dogs they have aren't even pit bulls, they're Staffordshire terriers." She shook her head. "No. *You* came back sometime yesterday and it was *you* who stole the money." She paused, breathing heavily. "And I bet you've got some of it on you. Go on, if you want to prove you're innocent, empty your pockets."

"Um," interrupted the principal, "we need to be careful here. There are privacy issues ..."

Matt jumped up. "I'll empty my pockets." He pulled out

his pant pockets. A pen came out, that was all.

"And the back pockets."

They were done and still nothing. He glared at her. "Do you want me to take my clothes off as well?"

The principal shot him a look. "Don't be rude, Matthew."

By then the smirking smile was gone from the woman's face. "Then it must be in his bag."

"Matthew," said Mrs Dingle, "are you prepared to let us search your bag?"

His bag had been hanging in the porch outside the classroom all morning. What if Cam had put something in it again? He took the risk. "Go ahead. You won't find anything."

Mrs Dingle opened a drawer in her desk and took out some rubber gloves, which she then put on. This would have been laughable if the outcome hadn't been so important.

The search took some time. When one compartment was found to be empty, Ms Williams would point to another. There were seven places altogether. Nothing was found other than his lunch and the book, still bookmarked at page five.

But none of that convinced Ms Williams. "All that proves is that he's smart enough not to bring the money to school. I still want him punished and I want the money back."

The principal took her time removing the rubber gloves before answering. "I need to think about this."

"If you don't do something," said the woman, "I'm going

to the police. I'll even go to the papers if I have to. I'm not having this swept under the carpet."

"All right," said Mrs Dingle, with a sigh. "I'll think about it overnight and let you know tomorrow. Will you hold off doing anything until then?"

The woman wasn't happy, but in the end she gave a reluctant nod.

"And you, Matthew," said the principal turning to Matt, "you also need to think about this overnight. The best thing you can do is admit your crime and bring the money to school in the morning. That will lessen your punishment. Now get back to class."

5

PUNISHMENT

At lunchtime, Matt went down to the caretaker's shed looking for Cam and Jay.

"Hi, Matt, " said Jay as if nothing had happened between them.

"Been helping any more little old ladies?" asked Cam.

Matt moved so that he was standing over them. "Did you steal her money?"

Cam stared up at him. "What money?"

"The money in the jar," Matt shouted. "The money you stole."

"That would be the money you never told us about," said Cam, calmly. "How could we steal it if we didn't know it existed?"

"You said you were going to her house."

Cam chuckled. "Matt, I was winding you up. We don't do houses."

For a few moments Matt stood there, beginning to feel stupid.

"Well, somebody stole it," he said, dropping to the ground.

"And I bet they're saying it was you," said Cam. Matt nodded. "So did you?"

"No!"

"Then tell us about it," said Jay. "Maybe we can help."

That took the next half hour.

"Did you tell anyone else?" asked Jay.

"Only my nana."

"Do you trust her?"

Matt replied without hesitation. "Yes!"

"Then someone else must have known about the money."

"The plumber."

"Yes," said Jay. "We need to find out who her plumber is. He could have told someone."

"Leave it with me," said Cam. "I have contacts."

"You need to do it quickly," Matt said. "Mrs Dingle is deciding my punishment tomorrow."

"Argh, don't worry about that," said Cam. "Ding-a-ling will stand you down, that's all. It's happened to me heaps of times. If you're lucky, you'll get some time off school."

Walking home that day, Matt thought of lots of things. His bad luck, his father, even thoughts questioning Nana's honesty. He'd told the others that he trusted her — but did he really know her that well? She was so poor that the thought of several hundred dollars lying around might be very tempting. Also, it seemed as if Nana and the old lady's daughter didn't get on too well. Maybe she stole it just to spite Sharon Williams.

When he reached the old woman's house, he stopped and tried to envisage Nana sneaking out of the house with the jar and running across the road to the empty section. No matter how much he tried, there was no way Matt could see her doing that. It had to be someone else. Crossing the road himself, he went to the bushes at the back of the section hoping to find some clues.

The jar was no longer there, which had him wondering whether it ever had been. Everyone was accepting Sharon Williams' story as if it were the truth. But what if she was short of money and had stolen the jar herself? Blaming Matt would be the perfect cover. There was no doubting she was mean enough to do something like that. Yet, although he searched for several minutes, there was nothing amongst the leaf litter that would incriminate her or anyone else.

Dinner that evening was very different to previous school nights. Nana had already had a phone call from Mrs Dingle, so she knew that side of the story. Matt now told her his.

Afterwards they had a discussion about Brayden Smith and why Sharon Williams had said, "Like father, like son." Matt knew some of the story, particularly the bit about how his father's dad had worked in the forests near Ruatoria and been killed when a log fell on him. Nana filled in the detail.

"Bray was always a bit wild," she said. "Ed was away in the forests for weeks on end and there was only me to try and control the three kids. The girls were mostly okay, but Bray was always in trouble at school. Nothing serious, just misbehaving all the time. Then Ed got killed. Bray was fourteen at the time, but he was big for his age and started mixing with older kids. Half the time I had no idea what he was up to. Then he got caught stealing a car for joyriding. I believe the older kids were using him because they all had previous offences and might go to prison if they got caught. Anyway, that was his first offence. We had a family group conference at the court and after that I kept a much closer eye on him."

She fiddled with the knife and fork on her empty plate, her mind clearly somewhere else.

"By then he was already mad about cars, and trying

to keep him away from them was impossible. Instead, I decided to make sure that he learnt about them in the right sort of way. I paid for driving lessons and courses on car maintenance. Eventually he got his licence and, when he was old enough, he got a place at the polytech doing panel beating — collision repair, they called it. For three years he managed to keep out of trouble."

Again the knife and fork were rearranged.

"Then he bought a car, and the real problem started. Cruising up and down the main street, burnouts, street racing. His car was impounded more than once. Each time he was disqualified from driving, which he just ignored. That went on until he met your mum. After that, things changed. You were born and they moved to Hastings. He became a good family man and everyone thought he'd grown out of all the racing stuff. Until he changed jobs and it started up again. Then … well … you know what happened."

Yes, Matt did know what happened. His father was charged with reckless driving so many times that in the end the judge decided time in prison might sort him out. He was sentenced to six months but would serve less than that. If he behaved, he'd be out in a few weeks, but he'd have no job, and the chances of getting another as a panel beater were not great. In the meantime Matt would stay with Nana, which, up until then, he hadn't minded too much. But that was sure to change unless he could sort out the stolen money thing. Matt was beginning to see that the meeting the next day could be one of the more important events in his life.

The dreaded call to the office came at 9:47.

Nana was already seated in the reception area when Matt arrived. She'd insisted on being present. Matt was pleased to see her, and also to see that Sharon Williams was *not* there. Maybe things wouldn't be too bad.

Mrs Dingle stood and shook hands with Nana before guiding them to some comfortable chairs in the corner. On the coffee table was a pitcher of water, glasses and a packet of tissues. After they'd both declined water, the meeting began.

"Mrs Smith, I gather you're familiar with the facts surrounding the stolen money?"

"I know that Matt was invited into a house where he saw a jar of money, and that later this money went missing. Those are the *only* facts, I believe."

"Not quite," said Mrs Dingle. "He was also seen coming out of an empty section where the money jar was later found."

"Doesn't mean he stole it."

"In my mind, it is very strong evidence that he did."

"Matt doesn't steal things."

Mrs Dingle's eyebrow's rose. "No?"

"No!" said Nana, without hesitation.

Right then, Matt knew what was coming next.

"Well unfortunately, that's not true," said the principal, shuffling through some papers. "Earlier this morning I rang his previous school in Hastings and they told me he was caught shoplifting at a local shop."

Nana turned on him. "Is that true, Matthew?"

He gave the slightest of nods.

"Now that you know about this other event, Mrs Smith, I'm sure you'll understand that I lean towards accepting that he stole the money."

Nana sighed. "So, what are you planning to do?"

"My immediate concern is for next week. At the moment he's down to go on a city camp to Auckland. That's now out of the question. I can't allow a known thief to go on a school trip that includes visits to shopping malls and other public places. The other Year 7 camp is in Hamilton where there will be similar temptations."

"You want me to keep him home all week?" asked Nana.

"That's one possibility, but there is also another." She paused to get their full attention. "Year 8 do adventure camps and one of those is at Lake Waikaremoana. The camp is virtually in the bush, well away from the general public. It is run by Mr Klineck. He's a part-time soldier — a territorial — and runs his camps along military lines."

Matt's stomach lurched. Mr Klineck, also known as Klink, was the teacher everyone feared. Cam and Jay were in his class and had plenty of stories about the man and his methods.

Meanwhile, Mrs Dingle was continuing: "… his sort of discipline will benefit Matthew. And I'm sure that being with older students, he'll be more willing to behave himself."

"Does it cost any more?" asked Nana.

"Yes, but we can waive that if you decide that this is the right way to go."

"And if he does this, what about the accusations of stealing?"

Mrs Dingle took a deep breath, exhaling slowly through her mouth. "I will inform Ms Williams of this action, though I'm not sure she'll accept this as adequate punishment. In fact, I'm certain she'll want an admission of guilt, and at least some of the money returned."

"That's going to be hard if he didn't take it, isn't it?"

"But if he did," said Mrs Dingle, "this week will give him a good chance to think about what he has done, and hopefully give us an honest answer when he returns."

Nana moved in the chair until she was facing Matt straight on. "Matt, are you prepared to accept all of this?"

What choice did he really have? None, of course. None whatsoever.

"Yes," he said, quietly.

And so his fate was sealed. In three days Matt would be at Waikaremoana, the lake that would control his destiny.

PART TWO

6

AZURA

When Matt entered Mr Klineck's room on Monday morning, it's true to say he was more than nervous — he was actually frightened. Sure, the man had a scary reputation, but more than that, it was like starting school all over again. The only two in this class that Matt knew were Jay and Cam, and he was beginning to think they might well be enemies rather than friends.

The class was quietly listening to the teacher when Matt cautiously opened the door.

"Ah," said Mr Klineck, "Matthew. Welcome to 8KN. Class, this is Matthew Smith from 7SG. He is joining us for our camp." A hand shot up. "Yes Melanie, what is it?"

"Why isn't he going with his own class?"

"None of your business."

"Because he's a thief," called out a girl from the back.

Mr Klineck glared at the girl until she looked away. He could have said something that might have made it easier for Matt, but chose not to. Instead, he showed him where to sit.

For half an hour Matt listened to the final instructions for the camp, most of them about things they were not allowed to do, rather than what they would be doing. Then the buses arrived and everyone filed out of the classroom, collecting their packs from the porch before heading to the front of the school.

"One moment please, Matthew," said Mr Klineck as Matt went to follow the others. After the others had filed out, he said, "Despite the many reasons why you're here, I will be fair with you. You behave yourself and we will get on well. Do anything wrong and I will come down on you like a ton of bricks. Do you understand?"

"Yes, sir," said Matt, stiffly.

"Good. Now go join the others."

All the other camps had multiple classes and buses. Klink's had one class, seven adults and one bus. In addition to Mr Klineck there was a teacher aide, Ms Edwards, and two parents who would do the cooking. The other three adults — two men and a woman — were dressed in khaki. Like Klink, they were part-time soldiers in the territorials. They were the instructors for the week.

By the time Matt arrived out front, they had everything

under control. He put his pack where they said, and stepped onto the bus to find there was only one seat left, and that was beside a girl.

Most girls at Oneroa Intermediate had longish hair, usually tied back in a ponytail. If the hair was short it was symmetrical and trimmed to frame the face. This girl's blonde hair was long on one side, and spiky short on the other. Also, since they were all wearing mufti, she was even more noticeable that day due to her long, flowing skirt, the very last garment you'd expect to see on an adventure camp.

"Hello," she said after Matt sat down, "I'm Azura. Welcome to Camp Ghastly."

Matt smiled. "Why do you call it that?"

"You'll see. Maddy, that girl who called you a thief, she and others will try to make your life hell. And when they do, don't expect any sympathy from Klink, he'll just tell you to toughen up."

"Sounds like you've had experience."

She grinned. "Heaps. Every day they try to get to me."

"Do they?"

"Nope! I just send myself to a different place where no one can touch me." She closed her eyes. "Which is what I'm going to do now. Nudge me when we get somewhere interesting."

For the next three hours Matt found no reason to nudge Azura. The bus followed State Highway 2 until they got to Wairoa, where it headed inland on SH38. The road surface changed to gravel and the rivers alongside got smaller — nothing Matt would call interesting.

Then they started climbing, almost too steeply for the ageing bus which groaned its way up the narrow road — it would have been faster to get out and walk. Just when it seemed that the bus would give up entirely, they reached a stretch of level ground by a turn-off. The bus turned and a couple of minutes later was moving alongside a tiny lake edged in green.

Matt nudged Azura. She opened her eyes. "Is this it? I thought Lake Waikaremoana was huge."

"This is Lake Whakamarino," he said, as if he knew everything, when he'd actually read it on a sign.

"And why is it interesting?"

"I think we're having lunch here."

They were. The bus drove around the lake to a grassy area by a large, concrete building. Before anyone could leave the bus, Klink laid out the boundaries and the rules for behaviour.

"You are not, I repeat not, to go anywhere near the power station." He pointed to the concrete building. "And that rule includes the walkway across the front. You sit down to eat your lunch and you put all rubbish back into your bags. Anyone not understand that?"

Matt thought about putting up his hand to say that nobody told him to bring lunch, but decided silence was the safer path.

Azura and Matt sat apart from the others with their feet dangling over a channel that carried water from the power station into the lake. The water was remarkably calm because the power station was not generating.

They had a sort of shared lunch. Matt shared his packet of bacon-flavoured chippies and Azura shared her salad wraps and fruit. The wraps contained beansprouts, alfalfa and other weeds. From the way Azura turned her nose up at the chippies, Matt wondered whether she was a vegetarian.

"These wraps would be nice with a bit of ham," he said, turning to watch her reaction.

Her eyes went wide. "No, they wouldn't. All that nitrite, sodium and cholesterol would kill you.

"Would taste great though."

She turned on him. "Why should a pig have to die for you?"

He slowly opened the wrap and took out a bean sprout, complete with seed. "What about this bean? It's going to die if I eat it."

"That's different. Beans are plants."

"It's okay to kill plants, but not animals?"

She turned away. "Forget it," she mumbled. And then, "I thought you'd be different."

Immediately Matt felt guilty. He'd been repeating almost

word for word the argument his father used to annoy vegetarians.

"Sorry," he said. "Thank you for the wrap. It's good."

Without speaking she began packing everything back into her bag. When she stood, Matt expected her to move away. Instead she said, "C'mon. Let's go talk to that fisherman."

The fisherman was down on the shore where the channel met the lake. He had all the gear: a hat advertising fishing rods, a vest with more pockets than Matt's school bag, and gumboots up to his thighs. Nearby was a bag for his catch.

"Caught anything?" asked Azura.

The man turned. "Nothing. They're not interested in feeding this time of day."

"Then why do it?"

He reeled in the line, leaning his rod on the bag. "Look around," he said, spreading his arms wide. "It's a lovely place to be on a nice day like this. Anyway, with the water so low, I thought the trout might be a bit hungry. Apparently not."

They looked around. The water in the lake was reduced to the size of a small river. On the far side was a large expanse of green dotted with black swans.

"Is that grass normally under the water?" Matt asked.

"It's not grass. It's water weed. *Lagarosiphon major* to be precise. It's a big problem around here. All of the smaller lakes are full of the stuff. DOC has its hands full trying to keep it out of Waikaremoana."

"Why is the lake level so low?"

"This has been a very dry summer. Waikaremoana is as low as the power company is allowed to take it." He pointed back towards the power station. "See the pipes coming down the hill behind there? They carry water from Waikaremoana, and they're the only way that water can get in here."

"What will happen to the fish if it dries up completely?"

"That would be a disaster. The fish would die. I'm sure it won't be allowed to get—"

"Do you eat the fish?" Azura broke in.

The man paused to take in both her tone and her clothing. "Yes. If they're a legal catch. Would you eat them?"

"No!"

"Why not?" he asked, tilting his head to one side.

Azura opened her mouth to answer, but before she could speak a voice came from behind.

"What ya catching, mister?" It was Cam swaggering up, the chain around his neck swaying from side to side. A few steps further back was Jay.

Again the fisherman delayed his answer to take in the person asking the question. He wasn't impressed. "Nothing at the moment. I was enjoying a conversation with these two."

Cam failed to notice the put-down. "Do you catch eels?"

"Occasionally one will take a lure. But I've not caught them around here."

"Are there eels here?" Matt asked.

"I believe so. The power company has a scheme of catching small eels down in the river by the bottom power station and shifting them up into the lakes. There's no way they can get up here by themselves."

"My dad says there are monster eels in Waikaremoana," said Jay.

"Yes, I've seen one or two up there. The Maori used to bring up elvers and release them for kai. Once they're in the lake there's no way out for them to return to the sea and breed. So they just stay there getting bigger and bigger until they either get caught or die. Some of them are over a hundred years old."

"I'm going to catch me one of those," said Cam. "Kill the slimy thing."

"Why?" asked Azura and the man together.

"Because they're slimy and ugly and ... and ... because I will."

"I suspect," said the man slowly, "that a hundred-year-old eel might be a bit smarter than you."

This time Cam didn't miss the put-down. His chin came out. "I *will* catch one. Where d'ya live, mister? I'll bring it and show you."

"I'm on holiday, which I gather you are as well." He turned to Azura and Matt. "School camp, is it?"

"Up at the lake," Matt said.

"Mmm. You must be the lot coming to Mokau Landing. A truck arrived this morning with portable toilets and other gear. You'll be just around the corner from me."

"Good!" said Cam. "I'll show you the eel when I catch it."

The man turned to him. "What's your name?"

Cam's chin protruded again. "Why do you want to know?"

"Cameron Nelson," said Azura, earning a scowl from Cam.

"Well take my advice, Cameron. Forget about catching monster eels. Any eels that still exist will be wily creatures. I don't see one giving up its life cheaply. They're huge things that could easily drag you into the water and that is definitely not a good place to be. Waikaremoana is not a lake to be messed with."

7

THE SUNKEN FOREST

Another hour and a half passed before the bus made it to their destination. Once they got up to the lake the view was scenic enough with blue-green water surrounded by rugged, bush-clad hills. But there was hardly anything else. Apart from a camping ground and visitors' centre, there were no buildings, farms or other signs of civilisation. Matt was beginning to understand why Mrs Dingle had sent him there – this was deep jungle, New Zealand style.

Waikaremoana has five big arms shaped a bit like the points on a star. There are also many inlets such as Mokau Inlet, which was their destination. The road mostly follows the shoreline, in many places carved into the rocks that rise almost vertically from the lake. At one of these they stopped.

"If you look to your left, you'll see Mokau Inlet," announced Klink.

Azura and Matt were on the left side of the bus and had a good view without moving. The other side had to stand and move to see, causing the bus to roll over onto its springs.

"Sit down!" yelled the driver. "Or we'll end up at the bottom of the cliff."

One glance downwards was enough to have them back in their seats. Directly below was the inlet, about half a kilometre wide. At the head, a piece of land jutted out, forming two bays. One had a river flowing into it through toetoe-covered flats. Across the river was an area that looked as if it had been mowed. Dotted around the edge were some vans and a couple of tents, with a concrete toilet block tucked behind bushes.

"Is that where we're staying?" asked a kid from the back.

"No. We're around the other side," replied Klink. "The bit you can't see from here."

Moving on, they crawled along the cliff face towards the end of the inlet. From there they crossed a narrow bridge and stopped again shortly afterwards so that Klink could do his tour guide bit. "Look back and you'll see Mokau Falls."

Matt looked and saw water pouring over a cliff face down into a valley.

"That's a forty-metre drop down to the bottom. Usually there's much more water than that, but they've had little rain here over the summer and all the streams are low. That bridge across the top is the one we went over a moment ago. See those rocks below the bridge? Normally, they're covered with water." Klink turned to the guy sitting next to him. "You know, Al, we could almost abseil down those falls in these conditions."

"Yeah!" said Al. "Easily."

"Can you get around to the bottom?" asked the same kid from down the back.

"With difficulty," replied Klink. "That tall grass down there is toetoe, otherwise known as cutty grass. It'll cut you to shreds if you're not careful."

Matt took it all in. Below the falls, the water became the river that flowed into the inlet. While he wasn't too sure about the abseiling bit, he did think that the river and bottom of the falls would be a good place to explore, cutty grass or not. For the first time he felt a touch of excitement about the camp. Perhaps it wasn't going to be so bad after all.

Setting up camp was done with military precision. Although each group had different shaped tents, all had to have their openings on the same side and be equally spaced from each other. The four girls' tents were at one end of the campsite, the boys' at the other. Separating the two groups were the adult tents, the cooking shelter and the washhouse. The portable toilets were well away from the tents, close to a couple of public toilets and an ablutions block. There were no showers.

Matt was added to Cam and Jay's tent, which also included a small, quiet kid called Paul. Matt would soon find out that Paul read a lot. If you asked him a question he would look up and answer, otherwise he would ignore everything that was going on around him. It became easy to forget that he was there.

After everything was set up to the adults' satisfaction, everyone was ordered to put on clothes and footwear suitable for a run through the bush. Few of the boys bothered to change, but most of the girls did, returning from their tents with a complete change of outfit. Matt noticed that Azura had chosen something sensible, even though it was still quite different to what the others wore.

Klink led the way, with a group of keen kids behind him. Cam and Jay had already said they were going at the back so they could dawdle instead of run. Matt joined Azura in the middle of the pack.

The track was obviously little used, with bare ground hardly wider than their shoes. Small branches arched over at head height, at times slowing the running to a walk. Matt didn't mind as it allowed him to keep up with Azura, who was a much better runner than he'd anticipated. She moved like a racehorse while he was more like a cow, lumbering along in her wake.

In places the path had to detour around the trunks of huge trees that stretched up and through the canopy of the undergrowth. Similar trees had been alongside the road, their tops filled with other plants and looking like gardens in the sky. They gave the landscape an ancient look that Matt had not seen before. He figured this must have been what most of Aotearoa would have once been like.

At the top, the bush gave way to toetoe, suggesting that the trees had been cut down, although there was no sign of why that might have been. Maybe at some stage it had been a pa, for it gave a great view over the lakes and the surrounding hills. Everyone stood taking in the vista while waiting for the stragglers to arrive.

Matt was gazing at the other side of the lake when Azura grabbed his arm.

"Look down there," she cried. "There're trees in the lake."

Beside them Klink chuckled. "Bet you've never seen something like that before. Take a good look because I've been here many times and never seen them as clearly as this. Must be a combination of a low lake level and the right angle of the sun."

The afternoon sun had most of Mokau Inlet in the shadow of the hills, but at a place below them the sunlight shone through the surface, allowing a view into the depths. And there were indeed trees down there, forming a sunken forest. Most were the remains of trunks with all signs of the tops gone. But a few still had branches and stood like strange creatures out of some dark fantasy story. The effect was awesome and a little scary.

"How did they grow under the water?" asked one of the boys.

"The water wasn't here when they grew," said Klink. He spread his arms to take in the lake. "The arms of the lake were valleys with streams that joined to form the river we drove alongside earlier today. Then, more than two thousand years ago, an earthquake caused a landslide that dammed the valley, forming the lake. Where we had lunch today was on part of that landslide. We'll take a closer look at it tomorrow."

"So the trees aren't growing?" asked another boy.

This was greeted with sniggers of ridicule. This boy was not known for his quick intelligence.

"No, Luke, they stopped growing two thousand years ago. The tops of them have rotted away because there's plenty of oxygen near the surface. But deeper down, the trees have been preserved. The lake's two hundred and fifty metres deep and not much oxygen can get down that far."

"Wow!" said Luke, and this time no one sniggered.

They stood in silence for a time, processing the information. It all made sense to Matt. He could easily visualise the scene without the lake: they would be on a high hill looking into a deep valley thick with trees, split only by streams flowing into the main river. A view that no human had ever seen because the earthquake came before mankind made it to Aotearoa, and yet, even though it had happened so long ago, the sunken forest had stayed around for them to see that day.

When they got back to camp they were ordered to take a swim. This was to be the way they would shower each day.

Once again, there were rules. No soap was allowed. If they wanted to give any parts special treatment then that could be done in the ablutions block. Togs had to be worn — not normal clothes — and everyone had to go in unless they had a very good reason, which had to be detailed in a note from a parent. Yet another thing Matt hadn't been told about.

Not that he wanted to get out of it, quite the opposite: water sports, and swimming in particular, were his thing. From the age of six he'd had lessons and regularly competed in age-group competitions, often winning. He'd not done any of that since moving to Gizzy, but was still in pretty good shape.

A track led from the campsite through a row of bushes and toetoe to a sandy beach. Lines of twigs and leaves showed that the water level was several metres lower than usual. They had to walk quite a way from the shore before the water was waist high; beyond that it dropped away more quickly.

Matt powered out into the deeper water before turning to see what the others were up to. Most were staying where they could keep their feet on the bottom. Only Jay and Luke were swimming out to where Matt was. Cam was back with the others, feet firmly stuck on the bottom.

Matt sensed an opportunity. "Cam!" he yelled. "Come out here." Cam acted as if he hadn't heard. "Cam! Let's go find that forest."

This time he responded. "Nah. Don't want to." He turned away.

By then Jay was alongside.

"Can't he swim?" asked Matt.

"Shhhh," hissed Jay. "Don't ever say that to him or he'll kill you." He glanced back to Luke. "And don't let anyone else know, either."

Matt nodded. Cameron Nelson, who always made out he was so tough and strong, had a secret weakness.

Luke arrived. "I'll come out to the forest."

"Okay. Are you coming too, Jay?"

"Nah, I'll go back to Cam."

"All right, let's go, Luke."

Only a small part of the inlet was still in sunshine, the rest being shaded by the hill they'd climbed. Matt headed for the sunny spot although it was probably beyond the 200-metre boundary that Klink had laid down. Anyway, how would he know if they were too far out? There wasn't a rope across or anything.

Luke was a good swimmer and Matt had to slow only a little to let him keep up. Matt could see shapes below, but nothing that he could swear was a tree.

When they reached the patch of sunshine, things became clearer. Branches were visible several metres down.

"I'm diving down for a closer look," Matt said when Luke was treading water alongside. "Can you duck-dive?"

Luke shook his head.

"You okay here? I won't be long."

This time Luke nodded.

Matt's longest free-dive was one minute, thirty-one seconds, but that was when he was doing swimming training. This day he doubted he'd be able to make a minute.

He didn't need to. The tops of the forest were not as deep as they appeared. Only a few seconds had passed before he was next to a ragged trunk, sharp at the end. He grabbed hold of it, wondering whether it was rotten or not. The surface was slimy, but hard. He tried to break a piece off the top to take back and show the others, but it was too tough. Looking deeper he saw a blurry branch stretching out from the trunk. Maybe that'd be easier — he'd need to take another breath first, though.

"How do you stay down so long?" asked Luke after he'd surfaced.

"That wasn't so long."

"We need to head back. Klink's waving his arms at us."

"Just a minute," said Matt, then took a breath and dived

before Luke had a chance to protest.

This time he swam below the treetop, down towards the branch. He was stretching his arm forward when it moved. At first he thought it must be rotten and swaying with the current. This idea was strengthened when it separated from the trunk. He took a couple of stronger strokes hoping to grab it before it sank.

But the thing didn't sink. Instead the end turned up towards him. A mouth opened. A huge mouth. One big enough to take in his arm.

Whether or not it was attacking, Matt had no idea. He didn't stay around to find out. He thrust away from the creature and powered upwards, breaking the surface so quickly that he nearly left the water.

"Swim!" he shouted "Swim! Gotta get out of here."

Luke might not have been the brightest of kids, but he could certainly identify panic when he saw it. He swam.

After fifty metres or so, Matt calmed and stopped, waiting for Luke to catch up. He'd had a chance to work out what he'd seen. That thing could easily have caught them. If its intention had been to eat them, it could have by now.

"What was it?" asked Luke gasping.

"An eel." Matt said quietly. "A humungous eel. The biggest eel there's ever been."

Luke's eyes went wide. "Godzilla!"

Matt chuckled.

"Not quite," he said. "But yeah, maybe God-zeel-la."

8

GALLEY SLAVE

By the time Matt and Luke got back to the beach, all the others were on shore, lined up, waiting.

Klink did not look happy. "How far out did I say the boundary was?"

"Two hundred metres," said Matt. "We didn't go that far."

Klink held up an instrument that looked a bit like binoculars except it had only one eyepiece. "According to my rangefinder, you were three hundred and twenty metres from this point."

Matt's head lowered. "Sorry. It didn't seem that far."

"Matthew, somebody who is as good a swimmer as you obviously are, would know the difference between two hundred metres and three hundred." He was right, but Matt wasn't telling him that. "I can understand Luke not knowing how far out you'd gone, but you must have known. As a punishment you're on KP duty tonight."

"What's that?"

"Kitchen Patrol," said Klink with a satisfied smile. "You do everything the cooks tell you to do. Now, go get changed and report for duty. Pronto!"

And so, while the others had free time, Matt worked in the kitchen tent taking orders from Kate and Lisa, two of the parents. The punishment could have been worse. Mostly it was peeling vegetables and doing dishes. The two women were good fun, except at the start when they made it obvious they knew he was considered a thief.

"See that?" said Kate when she was showing him the chiller. "That's a security camera. It records 24/7. With that we know who goes in and what they come out with. So, while you've got permission to go in, that doesn't mean you can take stuff. Okay?"

He was allowed to join the others for dinner. They were already sitting on the ground eating, having got their food while he'd been washing the cooking pots. He walked around, hoping that someone would ask him to join their group — no one did. Cam and Jay, who were talking to Luke, made it particularly obvious he was unwelcome. Finally he spotted Azura giving little waves from a quiet place under a tree.

"How's the food?" he asked, taking a seat. He thought it looked pretty good: sausages, mashed potatoes, carrots and peas with an onion gravy.

Azura thought otherwise.

"Klink promised Mum that they would have special food for me." She picked up some mashed potato with a fork. "This isn't special. It's the same as yours except there's no sausages. Where's the protein?"

"Do you eat eggs?" he asked. "I'm allowed in the kitchen. I could cook some for you."

"I do eat eggs, but it doesn't matter. I've got my own stash of protein that Mum made."

"Biltong and jerky?" he asked, smiling.

She kicked him in the leg. "Lentils and legumes. I'll give you some later, if you like."

"No thanks," he said, stuffing half a sausage in his mouth. "I'll stick to what my stomach knows."

After eating for a while she asked, "What did you find out in the lake when you went diving? You came to the surface as if you'd got a fright."

Matt glanced around. No one was looking their way. "I did. There was this huge eel, not far below the surface. Must have been at least two metres long."

"Did it attack you?"

"I'm not sure. It opened its mouth at me, but didn't have a go or anything. If it had, it could have taken my foot off, its mouth was so big."

"Don't tell Cameron — he'll want to kill it."

"I don't intend to. But I did tell Luke, and I think he might be telling them."

74

Azura looked over to where Cam and Jay were listening intently to Luke. "Then we'll have to stop him."

"I wouldn't worry," said Matt. "That fisherman was right. A hundred-year-old eel is going to be much smarter than Cameron Nelson will ever be."

After dinner, Matt had to return to the kitchen to wash the serving dishes. Meanwhile Ms Edwards read *Kidnapped* by Robert Louis Stevenson. She explained that it was an adapted edition with the 1886 language changed to the sort they would use. Fortunately she read loudly which allowed Matt to listen in too — so long as he didn't clang the dishes too much.

The story had a surprising amount of violence for a book read at school. Perhaps being set back in 1751 made the killing more acceptable. Matt didn't mind. He liked the story about David Balfour who, after his father died, was sent to live with his uncle. Ebenezer was a rich miser, having stolen the family fortune from Davie's father. He wanted nothing to do with Davie and arranged for him to be kidnapped. This part of the story was relevant to Matt's situation, as Davie Balfour was put on a ship and forced to work in the kitchen, known as the galley. Davie called himself a galley slave, which was pretty close to what Matt was at that moment.

Afterwards, back in the tent, Matt made an annoying discovery — his torch wasn't in his pack. Originally, Nana had organised everything, working from the list for the Auckland camp. She'd bought the things he didn't have and made sure that everything was fully named. Not having a Waikaremoana list, he just used the things that were already packed. He knew that there was a torch because Nana had complained about the price. He even vaguely recalled taking it out at one stage. Somehow the thing hadn't been put back. Either that or it had been stolen since they'd arrived at camp.

The only lighting around the camp was about twenty solar-powered garden lights standing on bamboo poles. Mr Klineck had warned them that they might run out of energy during the night and it could be very dark in the early hours of the morning. Without a torch, Matt had to hope that his bladder could last all the way through.

What Matt did find during his pack search was a pair of old racing goggles that would prove useful if he ever got the chance to dive down to the forest again. He put them in the pocket of his swimming shorts and headed to the toilet, determined to squeeze out every last drop before going to bed.

Paul was already reading by torchlight in his sleeping bag when Matt returned. Cam and Jay were still outside somewhere. Matt hadn't seen them since dinner. If he got organised quickly he could be in bed feigning sleep when they returned. That way he could avoid the eel discussion that had to be coming.

No such luck.

He'd almost drifted into sleep when a bright light shone

on his face, burning his eyes even though they were shut.

"Wake up!" yelled Cam, pushing Matt with his foot. "Wake up, galley slave."

"What do you want?" Matt replied, rolling over, shielding his eyes with a hand.

Both Cam and Jay were ready for bed. Cam was the one holding a large spotlight torch.

"A bedtime story," he said. "A story about that eel you saw."

Matt nodded slowly, playing for time. "So you've been talking to Luke. You don't want to believe everything he says."

"Then you tell us," said Cam. There was a menace in his voice that couldn't be ignored.

So Matt told them what he'd seen and how he'd first thought it was a branch. Then, when the thing opened its mouth, he took off. "That was it. That's all I saw."

"How long was it?" asked Jay.

Matt sat up looking for something to compare it with. Jay's sleeping bag was stretched out on a groundsheet. "Bit longer than that."

"Yeah!" said Cam. "And the mouth?"

"I reckon my foot could have fitted in it."

Another "Yeah" from Cam.

Jay shaped a circle with his hands. "So it was about this round?"

"Maybe a bit more."

"I can see why you took off.'

Cam turned and glared at Jay. "I can't. He should have stayed and fought it."

"Aw, come on, Cam," said Jay. "You can't fight something like that with your bare hands."

"Anyone with any guts would," said Cam.

Matt's face tightened. "That's unfair."

"Unfair? It's unfair to call you gutless?" He snorted. "We were watching. You came out of that water so fast, you almost took off. You were terrified. Frightened of an eel. You're a wuss, Matthew, and everyone there saw it."

"What would you have done?"

"Killed it. Killed it with this." He held up a red pocket knife.

"Hey," said Jay, "is that a Swiss Army knife?"

"Sort of. It's got a few tools but not hundreds of them."

"Where'd you get it?"

"From my brother."

"You steal it?"

"Nah," said Cam, glancing towards Matt. "He owed me." Eye contact was held for a moment, long enough for Matt to wonder why.

Jay went on. "Did *he* steal it?"

Another quick look at Matt before, "Got given it by the guy he works for."

"I thought he was still at school."

"Yeah, he is. One of his subjects is work experience."

"And he gets given tools?"

"Yeah, sometimes." Cam unfolded a blade of the knife. "This is what I'm going to kill the eel with."

"You'll never kill it with that," said Matt, who was still angry from being called a wuss.

"Will so," said Cam, sticking out his chin. "At least I won't run away from it like you did, wussy."

Matt snorted. "How are you going to get anywhere near it? You won't even get out there. You can't swim, Cameron. You go out that far, you'll sink to the bottom like a stone."

The moment he'd finished speaking, Matt knew he'd made a big mistake. All sound drained from the tent. Jay stared at Matt, wide-eyed. Even Paul stopped reading to look at him. But the reaction that frightened Matt was Cam's. He simply smiled, as if pleased with what had been said.

Seconds passed before he spoke. "Do you like being a galley slave, Matthew?" he asked quietly.

Matt said nothing.

"Do you?" This was louder.

"No."

"Well, you'd better get used to it, because you'll be doing a whole lot more of it before this camp is over. I'm going to make sure of that."

9

MONSTROUS EEL

Matt made it through the night without having to pee — just. There was enough light to make out shapes when he got up, unable to hold on any longer. It was probably around 5:30. He couldn't find out for sure as he didn't own a watch and his phone was at home. Mrs Dingle had said not to bring it as there was no signal around the lake. Whether the others had been given the same message, he couldn't say, but on Monday he'd seen several of the girls take out a phone and check the screen. Their reaction indicated there was no signal.

Having got up to pee, Matt decided to stay up and do the exploring that he'd planned for the previous evening. His sentence to slavery was over, so there was plenty of time before breakfast at 8:30. The thing was to make sure he was on time. He had no intention of being on KP again, despite what Cameron Nelson had threatened.

Mokau Landing had two separate public camping areas, one in each of the bays. The school had an arrangement with the Department of Conservation to take over the smaller one for the week. Their camp was separated from the other area by a ridge about 20 metres high. Although there were tracks over the ridge, on that morning Matt chose to follow the narrow vehicle access around the lake edge.

The many patches of yellowed grass suggested that the larger campground had been full over the holiday period. Now only three sites were in use: two campervans and one tent. One van was so run-down that it should have fallen apart before getting there. The other was more modern and could have been a hire vehicle. Only the tent had any fishing rods visible — that had to be the fisherman's. There was no sign of movement at any of the sites.

A walking track led from the edge of the lake up the valley alongside the Mokau River. Matt planned to take it all the way to the waterfall. As the sky lightened, birds began singing in the bush. He could recognise tui but none of the others. There were birds on the water too: ducks and black swans. Piles of droppings on the path suggested that was their night-time roost. A sign detailing regulations for anglers indicated the main reason for the path. Supporting this were the many scraps of fishing line tangled around the bushes.

After a few hundred metres the path narrowed as the riverbank got steeper. By then Matt could hear a faint roar which he took to be the waterfall. It sounded a long way off: too far away for him to get there and back before breakfast. He turned around.

Moving back past the sign he came across a family of swans in the water: a mother and eight fluffy cygnets. He found a place under a tree that was free of bird droppings and sat down to watch them feed. The mother would upend, stretching her long neck deep into the river. Some of the cygnets would try and copy, others would paddle around waiting for her to reappear. When she did, they would dive at her beak to get the weed she had dragged from the bottom. Fights would break out over the larger pieces.

This went on for some minutes before the mother spotted something in the water. She called her family in close before guiding them urgently downstream, away from the danger. By then Matt could see the surface being disturbed as something below swam across the river in his direction. As it got closer he could make out the snake-like dark shape of a very large eel. There was no way he could be sure it was the one he'd seen the day before, but he pulled his feet back from the edge anyway.

Upon reaching the bank, it snaked upstream a little before turning back. Then it went past him downstream a bit. Again it turned back. This time, instead of snaking past, the eel stopped. A black nose broke the surface with two tube-like nostrils pointing straight at Matt — the thing was sniffing him out.

The eel must have liked what it was sensing for it moved forward, pushing its head onto the bank. The most noticeable features were the thick lips surrounding a large mouth. In comparison, the eyes were tiny and Matt got the feeling that it couldn't see all that well.

For a time the head waved from side to side a couple of metres away, while Matt sat perfectly still. Surprisingly, he wasn't all that frightened; she seemed inquisitive rather than dangerous.

She? Why did he think of her as female? Probably the graceful movement. Nothing was rushed; everything was smooth and controlled.

Having worked out that Matt posed no threat, she began to wriggle forward. Now her actions became less graceful as she moved out of her natural environment. Her mouth opened and for the first time he felt a tremor of fear.

Yet still he stayed there, unmoving and silent, as she moved up alongside. She was easily twice as thick as his legs and about three times as long. A wriggle, bigger than the others, caused her to touch him. Immediately she stopped. Now she knew for sure that he was there. Her head moved until it was touching his thigh through the shorts. She stretched out until her mouth was right by the opening to the pocket. That was when Matt worked out what she was after.

Sausages!

The previous night after he'd finished the dishes, Lisa, one of the cooks, said he could take some left-over sausages and share them with others in his tent. He put two in each pocket and straight away forgot about them — until that moment.

"Wait," he said when the eel went to bite at the pocket.

At the sound of a voice, she stopped moving.

Matt fished a sausage out of the other pocket and, ever so slowly, moved it towards her head. Without warning, there was a flash of movement and the sausage had gone. He quickly pulled back before she tried another bite, not trusting her to tell the difference between fingers and food.

The place where he was sitting was on one of the lines of sticks and leaves left when the lake was higher. He picked up a short stick, skewered a second sausage and moved that towards her. Another flash and that was gone, but surprisingly not one bit of the stick.

The third sausage went the same way. He was organising the fourth when her head came up and swayed around as it had done earlier.

"She's detected me," said a voice.

Matt turned to see the fisherman from the day before standing behind him, dressed in fishing gear, holding rod and tackle bag.

"How long have you been there?" Matt asked.

"A couple of minutes. Long enough to be impressed by

your bravery and patience."

Matt shrugged. "She could've attacked me yesterday out in the lake, but she didn't. So I guessed she wasn't after me."

"I don't think she'd do much harm even if she did attack," said the man. "Her teeth are tiny things designed for gripping rather than cutting." He smiled. "I guess her reputation is much worse than her bite."

"Do you think she's a female too?" asked Matt.

"Yes, has to be. No male longfin eel could be that big. I'm amazed that any eel could grow to that size. She'd be a record, I bet. Forty or fifty kilos. I wonder if she'd let you pick her up."

Matt turned to the eel who had been moving her head as if listening, and stretched his arm out towards her body. The moment he touched her, he knew it was the wrong thing to do. Her body arched and twisted, whipping around on the grass until she was well clear, closer to the water.

"There's our answer," said the fisherman. "She doesn't want to be touched. I wonder if people have tried to catch her before."

"Sorry," Matt said to her, picking up the stick with the sausage. "Here, have this."

But she was not ready to forgive that quickly. He had betrayed her trust. A moment later she'd disappeared into the water. Matt got to his feet, disappointed that it had ended this way.

"You should try again tomorrow morning ... um ..." He looked at the boy expectantly.

"Matthew. Matthew Smith, but I like to be called Matt."

The fisherman stretched out his hand. "I'm usually called Satch."

"Satch?"

"Yeah, it's short for Satchmo — he was a very famous jazz musician."

That didn't make it any clearer.

"Look," the man went on, "I'd keep what happened here this morning to yourself. There's lots of people would like to catch a giant eel like that. There's one guy here I'm not sure about." He turned and pointed to the rusty van with the boat. "Him. I'm not sure what he's up to here, but I doubt that it's legal. He's already covered in prison tatts."

Matt nodded.

"And that boy yesterday — what was his name? Um ... Cameron Nelson. Don't trust him either. He'd want to kill it just to show that he could."

"He already knows that she's in the lake," said Matt. "Another boy told him after I'd seen her yesterday."

"Then you'll have to be extra careful if you return here. If she'll come out of the water for sausages, she'd be even more interested in red meat. I bet anybody could get her out with a bit of steak."

He left then, walking upstream in search of other fish. For a time Matt stood staring out at the water, hoping to catch a glimpse of the eel. There was nothing. If there hadn't been a glistening of slime on the grass, he could have thought it was all a dream.

But he knew it wasn't: it was one of the most magical things that had ever happened to him. He wanted more. And yes, he would be extra careful next time. No one, absolutely no one was going to hurt her. That was a promise he made, gazing out over the water. If necessary, he would guard her with his life.

10

EARTHQUAKES AND LANDSLIDES

The morning programme was skills development. Over three mornings, groups would rotate through kayaking, abseiling and bush-craft. That first morning, Group C, with Matt as a late addition, was down for two and a half hours of bush-craft, which involved learning about native animals and plants, a bit of geology, and map reading.

As much as he could, Matt stayed apart from the rest of the group to do some thinking. He wanted to come up with a name for the eel. After spending close-contact time with the animal he knew that anything like Godzeella was wrong. She might look like a monster, and she might chomp at food like a monster, but the way she came out of the water was so smooth and gentle that he couldn't give her a monster's name. If Godzeella was out, what should she be called?

Ceela? Eella? Heelen, Isabeel … Nothing seemed right.

Meanwhile, the group was wandering through the bush following the instructors who were pointing out different features: edible plants, insects that bite, rocks that could be used to make a spark … that sort of thing. Matt took some of it in, but mostly his mind was elsewhere, or rather eelsewhere.

When they got onto map reading, he had to stop thinking about names to concentrate more. That's when, out of nowhere, a name came into his head — Elsa. Well, not exactly out of nowhere for he knew where it came from. At his previous school they had read the book *Born Free*, a true story about a lion who was brought up by humans before eventually being returned to the wild.

Elsa was perfect. He wouldn't even alter it to Eelsa, and he liked the similarities between his Elsa and the one in the book. Lions were animals that scare people and yet in the story Elsa was shown as loving and mostly gentle. Eels were much the same: scary in form, with a bad reputation. Humans wanted to kill them just because they were carnivores or, like Cameron, to show how strong and tough they were. The Adamson family who raised Elsa the lioness had to protect her from poachers and big-game hunters. Matt knew that he would need to do similar things for his Elsa.

The afternoon programme every day was tramping. The one for Tuesday left from where they'd first seen the lake the day before. After lunch Matt filed into the bus making sure to be sitting next to Azura. He was dying to tell her about Elsa, but, knowing there were ears all around, held back. Instead they discussed the morning's activities.

Azura had learnt to abseil down a small bank. She was proud of her efforts, mostly because she'd not had many opportunities to do physical things before. Her parents were artists and everything they did together required creative skills, not physical. Her father was a sculptor well known for his wood carvings; her mother was noted for her watercolour paintings. Everything they did at home assumed that Azura would become a creative artist as well. She too thought it would happen, hoping to become a children's book illustrator.

All the time she was talking about her family, Matt was thinking how different his was from hers. The last thing he wanted was to follow in *his* father's footsteps, especially to where he was at that moment. His mother's career path wasn't all that interesting either; before she had kids she'd worked at many places, mostly as a waitress or a checkout operator, neither of which Matt wanted to do for the rest of his life.

Their conversation filled in the time as the bus trundled along the dusty road past the Information Centre to the top of the landslide that formed the lake. From there on, they made several stops so that the geology of the area could be explained. In many ways it was the geological story of New Zealand.

New Zealand is a country that is still growing, Matt learnt. Most of the mountains are still rising out of the sea. Generally this happens slowly, just a few millimetres per year, but sometimes there is a big jump, such as happens in earthquakes. The most recent big jump around Waikaremoana happened in 1931. It was called the Napier earthquake because that's where the most damage occurred, less than 100 km away from Waikaremoana. On 3 February that year, the land was lifted two metres out of the sea in just a couple of minutes, catastrophic evidence that New Zealand was still growing.

In the last five million years, through a combination of slow movement and earthquakes, some parts of the country have been lifted 20 km. And yet New Zealand doesn't have mountains that high — no country does. That's because there is another force operating: erosion, the wearing down of the mountains by water, ice and air. And, like the growth that forms the mountains, this decay is happening all the time, but it can also happen very quickly in the form of a landslide.

About 2200 years ago, an earthquake struck the east coast of New Zealand's North Island. No humans were around at the time to observe the event, but geologists are good detectives and have worked out what must have happened at Waikaremoana.

The start of the earthquake caused all the loose rock on a nearby mountain to come together in a large landslide that flowed into a valley where a decent-sized river had flowed for millennia. With the top of the mountain gone, there was less pressure holding the rest together. As the shaking increased, a monstrous slab of rock, kilometres long and wide, began sliding along the joins between the layers. When it hit the original landslide, it was travelling at close to 200 km/h. Major parts of the slab shattered into smaller pieces filling that part of the valley to a height of 400m. A natural dam had been formed, albeit a rather leaky one, because the large chunks of rocks couldn't make a good seal.

With the river blocked, the valley started to fill with water. So big was the dammed space that, even with the high rainfall in the area, it took more than twelve years to fill. Often natural dams like this burst shortly after the water begins to flow over the top. That didn't happen here, possibly because the huge rocks were too heavy for the water to move. The dam has survived for more than 2000 years and the lake is considered to be permanent.

Nowadays, the water rarely flows over the top of the dam. Instead it is taken away in pipes providing the energy for three hydroelectric power stations. When released 450m below, the water finally makes it into what remains of the river that was destroyed in just a few minutes a couple of centuries before the birth of Jesus Christ.

11

ONEPOTO CAVES

The tramp was on the Onepoto Track, a winding path across the part of the barrier formed by the sliding slab. They were to start at the northern end and travel south to where the lake used to overflow. Before beginning there was a 20-minute lecture about how everyone should behave, and the care they should take. Mr Klineck stressed that the tramp was a tricky one, but if everyone was sensible they'd all get through without problems.

Azura and Matt let most of the class rush off before slipping into the file with just three kids and two adults behind. Soon they were alone, the faster ones having moved out of sight ahead, and the slow ones left behind.

Despite the hot, sunny day, the track was cool and inviting, the surface cushioned by leaves from the overhanging branches. While there were none of the big trees seen on other walks, the undergrowth was thicker with many of the plants climbing over large, angular rocks. Matt could name only supplejack, the Tarzan-style vines that kids use as a swing.

As they walked, Matt told Azura about Elsa, describing her not as a monster, but as a gentle giant with rather clumsy eating habits.

"I must see her," said Azura when he'd finished.

"You will," he replied. "I'll take you to her before dinner. That's if she'll come back to the same place."

"What if she's out in the lake at that time, like she was yesterday?"

"Then I'll show you in the morning."

By that stage of the tramp, all noise from the rest of the class was blocked by the forest, leaving them to enjoy the sounds of nature that were all around: birds, cicadas, the creaking of branches in the soft breeze. Never before had Matt walked simply to enjoy the surroundings, but with Azura it seemed perfectly natural, her presence adding to his enjoyment.

At one stage she stopped, before guiding him off the track a few metres to the trunk of one of the bigger trees.

"Look at that," she whispered, pointing to a dark patch of bark.

At first Matt couldn't see anything more than a grey shape against the black of the bark. Then slowly the grey separated to reveal two brown wings patterned with red and white spots.

"It's a red admiral," said Azura, still whispering. "They're the most beautiful of our native butterflies."

"How did you see that from the path?"

She shrugged. "Mum and Dad are always seeing things that others miss. I guess I've learnt to do the same."

They watched as the butterfly slowly opened and closed her wings.

"I think she's feeding," said Azura. "That black patch is where sap is leaking out. She's drinking it."

Matt pointed higher up the branch. "So are they." Three yellow and black wasps were resting on another black patch.

"Arrgh," complained Azura. "I hate wasps. They're so ugly."

"Would you still think they were ugly if they didn't sting?"

She thought about that. "It's more than just stinging. Bees can sting but they're not ugly. Wasps are horrible things."

"My sister, Amy, is allergic to wasp and bee stings," said Matt.

"So is Maddy. She has an injection thingy that she has to use. The teachers have to carry it for her."

Matt nodded. "An EpiPen. Yeah, Amy has to use one too or she'll go into shock. She could die if she doesn't get injected."

"Same with Maddy," said Azura. "It must be tough in summer knowing that a single sting could kill you."

"Doesn't seem to worry Amy too much. It's just what happens in life. Our family has got used to it."

They continued the tramp. Within a few minutes, they had moved onto the main part of the landslide. Here the chunks of rocks were massive: double Matt's height and many times longer. There seemed to be no pattern to them. They lay at all different angles to each other forming a complex, three-dimensional maze.

Fortunately, there were orange markers to guide them — triangular shapes like ancient arrow tips, with the sharpest edge pointing the way. Mostly these were nailed to trees or to rough stakes in the ground, often in places that were not easy to find.

In the darker parts of the maze, the rocks were covered with mosses and ferns. At other points, the surfaces had been polished by the many bodies that had tried to squeeze through a narrow gap or climb over an annoying obstacle. Supplejack vines grew over some of the larger rocks providing helpful climbing ropes.

And there were caves. Not the sort carved out by running water, but the ones formed by stacking blocks on top of each other. Some you could pass through, others were dead ends.

"I feel like an ant," said Azura after one particularly difficult passage. "An ant climbing through a pile of Lego™

blocks after some kid has smashed his toy onto the floor."

Matt chuckled. "Yeah. I'm sure it would be easier with six legs."

"And if we could climb like Spiderman," added Azura.

Soon afterwards they made it through the worst part and took a rest in a small clearing. A single orange triangle nailed to a tree showed the route going to the right, towards the lake. However, a more obvious path led the other way. After some discussion they followed the marker.

That was a big mistake.

There was a path of sorts, but maybe not made by humans. Mostly they were walking blind, the view blocked by shrubs arching across at head level. For the first few minutes Matt led the way. Then Azura complained that he was letting the branches flick back into her face, so they swapped places. Now he was the one who had to duck flying branches. He slipped back a bit to make it easier, allowing Azura to move more freely.

They went like that for a few minutes before he heard a crash of breaking branches up ahead. A scream followed. Then "Matt! Help! Matt, help me!"

"Coming!" he yelled, moving cautiously forward.

Just as well he did. The so-called path simply ceased to exist. One moment he was battling his way through branches, the next he was teetering at the top of a bluff. Many metres below was the lake, edged with more of the huge blocks.

Luckily the cliff had enough cracks for plants to take root. About a metre below the lip was Azura, her arms wrapped around a thin trunk, the toes of her shoes gaining some support on a narrow edge a little lower down.

"Hurry, Matt, " she cried when she saw his head over the top. "I don't think I can hold on for long."

"All right." Matt tried to keep the panic out of his voice. His first thought was to lie down and see if he could reach her. It looked too far, but maybe, if she could reach up a bit …

He gave it a go, only to find that his hand was less than half the way down. No matter how much she stretched she wouldn't be able to make up the distance. What was needed was a rope, but there was no chance of finding one of those around.

Supplejack! The vines were everywhere. One of those would do.

But on looking around, he found they weren't so common in that part of the forest. He had to move quite a way back down the track to find one.

"Matt!" called Azura. "Where've you gone?"

"I'm getting supplejack."

"Hurry!" There was no mistaking the fear in her voice.

Hauling at the vine, he managed to pull several metres out of the tangle of undergrowth. There was more than enough to reach Azura, but could he pull her up?

Back at the cliff top he doubled the vine over to form

a loop which he fed over the edge until it was within her reach. "Okay," he said with a confidence he didn't feel. "I'll be able to pull you up with this, but you're going to have to let go of the trunk, and grab the vine."

"I don't think I can."

"One hand at a time. You can do it."

On her third attempt Azura got her left hand on the vine. After that the right hand was easy. She'd done her bit. Now Matt had to do his.

Grabbing both strands of the loop, he took up the slack until Azura was stretched out, her hands on the vine, her toes still on the ledge. To move any further he would have to support all her weight. He braced himself and pulled.

Although the edge of the rock cut worryingly into the vine, eventually it moved enough for Matt to know that Azura's feet must now be off the ledge, and she'd be dangling like a trapeze artist. Next he had to get her to the top and then over the edge.

Raising her up was relatively easy. There was enough friction between the rock and the vine to adjust his grip without her falling back. Soon he could see her hands just below the edge. If he could tie the vine around something then he'd be able to reach down and grab her.

Unfortunately supplejack is not as flexible as its name suggests. Certainly not supple enough to tie it tightly around the narrow trunks nearby.

"Hurry," cried Azura. "This is scary."

Then Matt had another thought: maybe he could wedge the vine between two blocks of rock. If done at one of the knobbly joints then it might stick in place.

It did! Again the rock cut into the surface, but it seemed to hold. However, just in case it failed, Matt made sure one foot was always on the vine as he shuffled back to the edge. There, he knelt, one knee on each strand and lowered his arm.

"Can you grab me?"

"I'll try."

For an agonising time, nothing happened. Then, just as he was about to take a look, his arm jerked as her hand grabbed his wrist. He pulled up until he could grasp her wrist with his other hand, which gave enough support for Azura to scramble her feet up the surface until she could bend her torso over the edge.

A moment later she was sprawled on the surface: exhausted, but uninjured and safe.

12

THE SEARCH

Back at the clearing, Matt studied the orange marker that had caused the near disaster. Two nails were intended to hold the metal in place. Somehow, the head of the top one had pulled through and was no longer effective. The other was loose, allowing the arrow to spin around until it was pointing in the opposite direction. While he found it hard to see how this could have happened without human help, he said nothing to Azura, who was still shaking from the experience. Instead he spun the marker to face the right way and jammed it in place with a small stick.

The rest of the tramp was not particularly exciting. At one place they found a pipe that had been drilled into the ground. The sign alongside said that concrete grout pumped down the pipe had helped seal some of the leaks in the natural dam, thus allowing more water to be used to make electricity.

A few minutes later they made it to the end. The rest of their campmates were sitting in the shade near the bus, which had travelled along the road while they'd been walking.

"You took your time," said Klink.

Before Matt could answer, Azura said, "We were looking at insects and things. We saw a red admiral and some wasps, didn't we, Matt?"

He nodded.

"All right," said Klink. "Take a seat in the shade. There's still another five on the track somewhere."

Matt sensed he was worried, and was about to tell him about the problem with the marker, when Azura grabbed his arm. "Over here, Matt. "

When they were seated Matt asked, "Why didn't you tell him about the orange marker?"

"You don't tell that man anything unless he asks. He'll just twist it around and use it against you."

So they sat and waited like the others. Most were sitting in groups chatting quietly. Cam, Jay and Luke were the only ones making a noise. They would talk quietly for a few minutes and then Cam and Luke would burst into raucous laughter. A couple of times they looked over to Azura and Matt as if they might be the cause of their amusement.

Matt was surprised to see Paul sitting in the same

group. He was reading, as usual, and taking no part in their discussion. It looked almost as if he was their prisoner or something.

As time passed, Klink and the other adults became increasingly agitated, looking at watches, and pacing back and forth. Clearly something had gone wrong. When Klink picked up a first-aid kit to study the contents, Matt figured he knew what the problem might be.

"Can you see Maddy?"

"No. Don't want to," replied Azura.

"She's not here. What if she went the wrong way and got stung pushing through the bush?"

Azura was silent.

"I'm going to tell him about the sign," said Matt, climbing to his feet.

"Don't, Matt. It'll only cause trouble. You don't know him the way I do."

Looking back afterwards, Matt was unsure what motivated his move. Perhaps he was hoping to get on the right side of the man. Whatever it was, he went over and told the adults about the orange marker and what had happened to them.

Of course they quizzed him about where it had happened, and that was when he volunteered to show them. After that, they stepped away and talked quietly for a time. When they split up, Al went over to the bus while Klink returned to Matt.

"I hope you're telling the truth, Matthew."

"I am."

Klink studied him for a while. "All right. You better show Al and me where this happened."

Al returned with a couple of packs which Matt guessed contained emergency equipment. Shortly afterwards they were on their way.

The two men had long legs and could cope with the rough terrain much better than Matt, making it difficult for him to keep up. Twice they had to stop and wait.

"You need to do more leg work, Matthew," said Klink. "Your upper body is great but you walk like a cow." He then illustrated by exaggerating the wobbly walk, swaying from side to side as he moved along the path. Al laughed, encouraging even more wobbling. Klink swayed so much that the phone case attached to his belt knocked a tree and fell off.

"You dropped your phone," said Matt, bending to pick it up.

Klink took it back, opened the case, removing the device. After pressing a few buttons he said, "Still works."

"Is there a signal around here?" asked Matt.

Klink smiled. "This phone gets a signal anywhere. It's a satellite phone. Here, have a look."

The thing was bigger and heavier than usual. A thick aerial protruded from the top.

"How much do they cost?" Matt asked, handing it back.

"Not so much to buy, but a lot to use. Calls are thirty bucks a minute on this one."

"Is it yours?"

"No. We've rented it for the week. We need something in case we have an emergency. The Board of Trustees insists." He turned to Al. "As if something might happen that we couldn't handle." They then both laughed at the impossibility of this before moving on.

At the small clearing the orange marker was back pointing the wrong way again — Matt's quick repair hadn't lasted.

"That's been done intentionally," said Al, examining the marker.

Klink nodded. "But it must have been done after all but the last came through or we'd have more missing."

"It was done when Azura and I came through."

Klink stared at the boy for a time without speaking.

"It looks like a group went the wrong way," said Al, heading in that direction.

"Then let's go find them," said Klink.

Many of the bushes through which Azura and Matt had struggled were now more broken than before. This made the passage much easier, and the clifftop more visible.

"This is where Azura fell over," said Matt.

They stopped and looked over the edge and around the place where there had so nearly been a disaster.

"And you pulled her up using supplejack?" said Klink.

"Yes."

"So where is it?"

Matt looked around. "I left it here on the ground."

Again Klink stared at him. "Yeah, Matthew, I'm sure you did."

"Maybe they took it with them."

Al snorted. "Yeah, right."

That was the moment when Matt began to think Azura had been right when she'd said not to tell.

Further around from the clifftop, any suggestion of a path petered out to nothing. And yet the broken shrubs indicated people had passed that way, so they continued.

The two men began calling. "Coo-ee! Coo-ee!"

Five minutes later they heard the first answer. Another two minutes and they could see them sitting on slabs by the side of the lake.

Seeing them and getting to them were two quite different things. They had pretty much slid down a steep slope to get to the lake's edge. If they'd stayed up top, their rescue would have been much easier. As it was, by the time all three kids and the two adults were back up top, almost an hour had passed.

The hardest to get up was Maddy. Matt found her to be a whiner who would do little to help herself. He would soon find that she was also vicious when under threat.

While they waited for everyone to catch their breath, Ms Edwards, the teacher with the group, explained what happened. "Maddy was out in front by herself. 'Checking the way,' is what she called it." She paused to give Maddy a smile.

"Anyway, when we got to the clearing, she wasn't within sight, so we called out. She answered from up this direction. 'This way!' she said. Well, even though the marker pointed that way, we weren't too sure, but in the end we decided that it was better to stay together as a group. By the time we caught up with her, she was already down at the lake. So we went down and joined her. I guess we should have stayed up here, shouldn't we?"

"Yes," said Klink. He turned to Maddy. "Did you see any sign that anyone had come this way before you?"

"No! But this was the direction the sign said, so it had to be right."

"You didn't see any supplejack on the path by the cliff top?"

"Supplejack?"

"The climbing vine that you see hanging everywhere. Matthew said he left some there."

Her eyes narrowed. "Nah. I saw nothing like that."

"Did you see any other people?"

"Not on this track. But before we took the wrong turn, when I was climbing over that really big rock I could see down into the clearing and I saw Matthew down there."

Matt held his breath, knowing what would come next, but hoping he was wrong.

"He was by the marker. I think he was fiddling with it."

Matt let out his breath. "I was trying to put it—"

"Quiet, Matthew," said Klink. "You'll get your turn to

speak later." Then to Maddy. "Did you see Azura?"

"No, only Matthew."

"Did you see any sign of anyone else?"

"No."

"And when you got to the clearing, you took the wrong path."

She stuck out her chin. "How was I to know it was the wrong path? I didn't think anyone would be stupid enough to change the sign around."

"Precisely," said Klink, climbing to his feet. "Okay, we'd better get back to the others." He turned to Matt. "We'll have a full investigation when we're back in camp. In the meantime, Matthew, you need to think about what you're going to tell us. Will it be the truth, or just more of your lies?"

Back in camp, they were arranged in alphabetical order and told to sit in rows under the trees. The investigation would replace the swim and free time; a punishment Klink justified with: "In a group, everyone is dependent on the actions of all others. It only takes one idiotic act for everyone to suffer." What he was really saying, was, *I'm doing this to make sure you all hate whoever's guilty, and I give you my permission to pick on him, her or them.*

Despite what had been said during the rescue mission,

Matt still had some hope that the real offenders would be found. This hope rested on the fact that Azura could back up his story. He also felt sure that Maddy was lying and thought this would become obvious to the investigators during the questioning.

The effect of being seated in alphabetical order was that they sat mostly in silence as few friends were sitting next to each other. Azura and Matt were at opposite ends of one row. Of the people Matt knew, the only two together were Luke and Cameron, performing like they had at the end of the tramp. Once again, much of their sniggering seemed to be directed in his direction.

One by one, Al called them into the tent where Klink and Ms Edwards sat in judgement. This time the sequence was not alphabetical, but rather in the order in which they'd finished the walk. This was done so that they could determine when the marker was vandalised. Once a person had been interviewed they were not to speak to anyone still waiting. Instead they had to return to their tent and stay there until dinnertime — yet more punishment of the innocent majority.

Slowly the number of kids sitting under the trees dwindled down to Paul, Cameron's gang, Azura and Matt, plus the three who'd got lost. Jay was questioned first, followed by Luke, and then Cam, who was in there for longer than any other person.

Matt's hopes rose.

Then Cam came out wearing a big sneering grin, swaggering his way towards the tent. Matt's hopes died.

Paul was next. He was in for less than a minute. When he came out he made a point of walking past Matt. "Sorry," he said without making eye contact. Matt knew then that he was in serious trouble.

Azura took longer. When she was finished, Matt tried to will her to look in his direction. Instead she marched off to her tent, staring straight ahead, as if he didn't exist.

When Al came out, Matt stood, expecting to be next.

"No," he said. "It's not your turn yet. You can wait."

Soon there was only Maddy and Matt left on the grass.

Finally, he got the call.

The two teachers were seated behind a picnic table. Al stood to one side, like a jailer.

"Well, Matthew," began Mr Klineck, "have you thought about what I said earlier? Are you going to tell us the truth?"

"I've already told the truth."

"No. You've told us a lot of lies, which you obviously thought we'd be stupid enough to believe."

"What I said was the truth."

He leaned back in the chair. "So you're sticking to that same story — that you and Azura followed the marker pointing to the right; that Azura fell over the ledge and you then rescued her. That's the truth, is it?"

"Yes."

"Then how come Azura knows nothing about it?"

That shook him.

"You'd think," continued Mr Klineck, "that if Azura had almost died, she'd remember it for the rest of her life. But in" — he looked at his watch — "three hours, she's already forgotten? That doesn't seem reasonable, does it?"

Matt decided to stay quiet. There was nothing he could say that would change Klink's mind.

"Did you know, Matthew, that police frequently film people who hang around a crime scene. It's well known that criminals often want to see the effect that their crime has on others. That's especially true of people who light fires. This thing was your fire. You vandalised the marker so that it faced the opposite direction. Then, when you got back to the bus, you wanted to see what had happened to those you had tricked into going the wrong way. So you came and told me that story about you and Azura. I suspected then that it was a lie. If it had been the truth, Azura would have come up with you and supported your story. Instead she kept well away from me, probably because the story you'd told her to tell was too crazy to be believed. However, I went along with the story as I knew it would be the quickest way of finding the missing persons. And I was proved right."

He took two deep breaths, letting each out slowly. He was about to pass judgement. "This is a crime we cannot treat lightly. That story about somebody going over a cliff could actually have happened because of your actions. We were extremely lucky that no one was hurt this time. But if it were to happen again, we might not be so lucky. You were sent to this camp to keep you away from the temptation of stealing. And yet now you're in trouble for something else and it has become my task to keep you away from the temptation of doing it again. I could send you back to Gisborne, but I don't think you'd learn anything that way. Instead, you will not go on either of the two remaining tramps. Each afternoon, from the end of morning activity until bedtime, you will assist the cooks in the kitchen. You'll do whatever they ask you to do. If you're not prepared to do that, then I will contact school and arrange for someone to come and collect you. So … what will it be?"

At first Matt was tempted to take option two: to return home to Gisborne, away from all the troubles of the camp. Not just to get away from Klink, or Cameron Nelson and his gang, but to escape from Azura, who, until a few minutes ago, he'd considered a friend.

Only one thing held him back. Elsa. He wanted to see that eel again, and so he made yet another decision that would affect the direction of his life. He looked Klink directly in the eyes and said that he'd stay.

13

ALONE

No teacher ever publicly named Matthew Smith as the person responsible for messing with the orange marker, but of course everyone knew. The only public announcement was that evening during dinner when Mr Klineck interrupted the eating by ringing a bell.

"As you know," he said in his most official voice, "we had a serious incident on the tramp today. One of the orange markers was vandalised so that it pointed in the wrong direction. The consequences could have been a disaster. Thankfully, due to the wise actions of those who went the wrong way, no one was harmed. But it might have been very different. Very different indeed."

He paused to let his eyes scan the whole class.

"Thank you for the help you gave in our investigation.

I'm sure that all except one of you will be pleased to know we've identified the culprit. The exception will be the criminal himself. He will now be subjected to a substantial punishment. This includes missing out on the two remaining tramps so that his offence cannot be repeated. Instead, he will do general camp duties." He smiled. "I'm sure we can find some really unpleasant ones for him. That's it — you may resume eating."

During all of this Matt sat outside the main group with his eyes fixed on the teacher. He sensed others turning and looking, but refused to make eye contact. He could have feigned regret for his actions, but how could he be truly remorseful when he'd done nothing wrong.

He was not the only one sitting alone. Nearby was Paul, with a book as usual … except, although he was looking down at it, no pages were turned. Further away was Azura, picking at her meal. Maybe she was the one feeling remorse, but as Matt could not see her face, he couldn't tell.

Like Azura, Matt had a vegetarian meal. He fished the meat patty out of the hamburger and put it in a plastic bag he'd picked up in the kitchen. This would be Elsa's breakfast. He was happy to go hungry if the reward was to meet with her again.

When the meal was over, the reading from *Kidnapped* continued. Davie Balfour was no longer a galley slave. Instead he was a hunted person, wanted for his part in the murder of a Highland chief nicknamed the Red Fox. Except

Davie was innocent, having played no part in the killing. Once again Matt was struck by the similarities between Davie's plight and his. The difference was that Davie Balfour had a friend — the Scottish renegade Alan Breck — whereas Matt had nobody.

That night was the longest ever. Matt's mind wouldn't let the day's events go. Round and round went his thoughts. At one stage he was convinced there was a major conspiracy operating, which involved almost everyone, particularly Cam, Luke, Jay, Paul, Maddy and Azura.

However, as time passed his thoughts became more rational. Luke was the sort of guy who'd join any group if they just gave him some attention; he wasn't naturally bad, not in the way Cam was. And Maddy's type looked for opportunities to be nasty; when Klink said Matt had left some supplejack on the cliff top, she said the opposite just to get him into trouble. Matt was willing to bet that the supplejack had been kicked over the edge.

The person who still worried him was Azura. She'd been such wonderful company over the first part of the tramp. He couldn't imagine her joining Cam to get him into trouble. There had to be another explanation, but no matter how much he thought about it, nothing sensible came to mind.

Ignoring a filling bladder is not easy when you're having

trouble sleeping. As the night wore on, the pressure kept building until Matt had to do something about it or he'd wet the bed. By that time the solar lights had used up all their stored energy and the tent was so black he didn't know whether his eyes were open or not. He could locate Jay and Cameron from their sleeping noises. Paul, however, was silent. Only when Matt sat up did he stir.

"Do you want my torch?" he whispered.

"Yes, please."

A moment later a reddish glow filled the tent: red, because the light was filtered through a hand held over the front reducing the brightness.

"I'll come too," said Paul, climbing from his sleeping bag.

Outside, there was almost enough light from the stars to see without the help of the torch. Matt had never seen so many stars. In places of the sky they were so thick that the individual dots merged into a glowing mist. A morepork called from nearby. Further away some unknown animal shrieked.

Instead of leading the way to the portable toilets, Paul headed off the grass into the bush.

"As long as we spread it around, our urine will do more good for the forest than it will dumped in a sewage farm," he explained.

That was the longest sentence Matt had heard him say. Taking a chance that he wanted to talk, Matt asked, "Why did you say 'sorry' when you came out after being questioned?"

Only when they were finished and walking back to the tent, did Paul answer. "Because I saw what happened to that marker and didn't say anything."

Matt waited for more.

"I was behind Luke and Cameron. When they got to that clearing, Cameron went straight to the orange marker. He used that Swiss Army knife to pull the marker away from the nail and then made it face the wrong way."

"Was he trying to get us lost?"

"No. He thought you were further ahead. He wanted you to be blamed when others got lost."

"Did he know you'd seen him?"

"Yes. At first I thought I was far enough back, but a bit further along I found him waiting for me. He threatened me with all sorts of things if I ever told."

"What? A bashing?"

Paul stopped and turned around. "No, nothing violent. It's always annoying stuff, like he'll hide my bag so I'll spend ages after school trying to find it. He'll tip everything out of my pencil case into somebody else's bag. Once, he ripped the last chapter out of the book I was reading." A pause. "I suppose now you're angry with me for not telling Klink."

"No," said Matt softly, and it was true. He'd had enough contact with Cameron to know what he was like.

They resumed walking. Back at the tent Matt hesitated: what was the point of returning to bed? He wouldn't sleep.

"What time is it?"

Paul shone the torch on his watch. "Five eleven."

Close enough to morning to get up. "Hey, can I borrow your torch? I'm going for a walk."

"Sure," said Paul without hesitation. "Can I come too?"

After pulling on some clothes they set off for the other camp. In Matt's pocket was the meat patty from dinner. Although feeding Elsa with Paul around would be a bit of a risk, he wasn't too concerned. In fact, he was starting to feel a common bond with this rather strange boy — both were victims.

The better of the two vans had gone, leaving only Satch's tent and the wreck owned by the guy who Satch claimed was covered in prison tattoos. That was was good, Matt thought, as it reduced the chance of other people discovering Elsa's hiding place.

Matt waited until they were sitting by the tree near Elsa's home before telling Paul why they were there. Paul knew about the eel from the conversation in the tent. The news that the eel was now a friend and they were about to feed it got him quite excited — and a touch scared. Matt said nothing when he edged further up the bank, away from the water.

They waited ... and waited.

In an attempt to attract her attention, Matt even put a scrap of meat right by the water's edge.

As dawn broke, the swan family appeared from further upstream along with a group of small ducks. Maybe this would trigger Elsa's arrival as it did the first time.

Nothing.

While they waited, Paul talked about school and his experiences. Like Matt, he was reasonably new to Gisborne, his parents having moved from Auckland during the previous year. He'd already had a full term of coping with Cameron Nelson. He said he dealt with it by imagining what he'd do if he ever got the chance of revenge. Most of these fantasies seemed to involve science fiction: Cameron would be zapped to some terrible planet where non-human creatures would do all sorts of things to him. One of his favourites was the Planet of the Xargs. This was inhabited by intelligent reptoids that would make Cameron work as a slave, which, according to Paul, mostly involved cleaning their toilets.

They began inventing all sorts of fun planets with fantastic creatures that would punish Cameron for the way he'd behaved on Earth. So much fun that neither noticed things were happening in the water until a duck let out a loud squawk, flapping furiously towards the opposite bank. Looking up, Matt saw that the mother swan and her cygnets had already gone. The remaining ducks had parted to leave a clear waterway between the lake and the tree.

This was Elsa's pathway.

"Look along there," whispered Matt. "That's where she'll come."

"No," Paul whispered back, pointing to the water's edge just beyond their feet. "She's already been. The meat's gone."

It was too. Matt shook his head, amazed that she could have got it from right in front without them noticing. He broke off another piece and put it on the grass between their legs. "She won't get that without us seeing."

Soon afterwards, a dark, glistening shape eased out of the water, the head moving around sensing the air for food. Paul eased himself sideways, further away from the meat.

"Stay still," said Matt. "She won't hurt you."

"You sure about that?"

On hearing their voices, Elsa stopped moving to assess the danger. When convinced there was none, she gave two sizeable wriggles, enough for most of her body to be out of the water.

Paul gasped. "She's huge!"

Matt nodded. Even though he'd seen her twice before, he still found her size amazing.

With a slight stretch of the body and a turn of the head she eased the meat into her mouth. Only then did she do a chomp and it was gone. Another piece went the same way.

"Feed her with your hand," said Paul.

"No way! You haven't seen one of her real chomps yet."

"I'll do it. Give it here."

Matt turned and looked at him. His eyes were bright, his whole face alight with excitement. This was far from the scared person from a moment before — he had fallen under the Elsa spell.

"All right," said Matt, handing over a bigger piece, "but don't blame me if you lose your fingers."

Taking the piece, Paul held it out, closer to his body than the other pieces had been. Then he began moving it around as if trying to hypnotise her. And it worked. Elsa began swaying in time with his movement. This dance became slower and slower until Paul's hand was still. Elsa stopped too. Then she opened her mouth, leaned forward and lightly took the meat from his fingers.

"Yes-s-s," hissed Paul. "She's magic."

There was enough patty left for two more bites. Matt let Paul do them both so he could sit back and simply watch this incredible animal.

Then it all went wrong.

Before Elsa had finished the last piece, her head went up — the same as it had when Satch had approached. A smile began to form as Matt swivelled around, expecting to see him again.

Then the smile died and he turned away.

"Hi Azura," said Paul. "You're up early this morning."

14

REVENGE

Elsa had gone. Azura had not.

Paul was raving on to her about how incredibly fantastic the experience with Elsa had been. Matt was staring at the water, not to see anything but to show he was ignoring Azura standing behind.

Was he sulking? Yes. He'd readily forgiven Paul for not telling the truth, and yet he was trying to punish Azura for doing the same. Not that it seemed to have any effect on her. She too was excited about Elsa. She'd caught the last part of the feeding and had been amazed at how gracefully the eel could move. They went on and on about it until Matt lost his cool.

"Why did you do it?" he yelled.

Paul looked at him, shocked. "Do what?"

Azura lowered her head — she knew what.

"Why did you lie?"

"Because it was the best way."

"Best for who? For you? So I'd get into trouble and you wouldn't."

"Klink was always going to blame you, no matter what I said. If I'd told him about falling, he would have claimed that's what you told me to say."

She was right about that. Matt began to calm a little. "But why was that the best way?"

"Because only you have to do KP. If we're going to get revenge we need one of us free to keep an eye on Cameron and his lot."

"Revenge?" said Paul and Matt together.

Azura nodded. "Yes. It's time to make Cameron Nelson pay for his actions."

"That could be dangerous," said Paul.

"I know, but if we don't do it, he'll just keep making our lives hell."

"Do you have a plan?" asked Matt.

She sighed. "No. I was awake half the night trying to think of something."

"I have a plan," said Paul.

Matt snorted. "What? Zap him to the Planet of the Xargs?"

Ignoring that, Paul fished into his pocket. "It involves this." His hand opened to reveal one of the orange markers.

"You stole one?" said Azura.

"Not me. Cameron." He went on to tell what happened.

After threatening Paul about the reversed orange marker, Cameron had forced him to stay with their group so they could keep an eye on him. At one stage Cameron stopped and pried another marker off a tree and this one he put in his pocket. When Luke asked why, Cameron said it was a backup plan.

Paul had to stay with them even after the tramp was finished and they were waiting for the rest of the party to arrive. When it was clear that people had been tricked into going the wrong way, Cameron took out the marker and threw it into the bush, saying, "Don't need that now."

"What were you going to do with it?" Luke had asked

"If nobody had got lost, I was going to put it in Matthew's pack and tell Klink I saw him steal it."

Later, after the search party had left, Paul had managed to sneak into the bushes and retrieve the marker which now lay on the grass between them.

"How do *you* plan to use it?" asked Azura.

"Much the same as Cameron would've, except I'll put it in *his* bag, so that it gets found when they search it."

"Why are they going to search his bag?" asked Matt.

"Because Cameron will be caught stealing something else."

"What's he going to steal?"

"That's the part I haven't worked out yet."

"He's stealing stuff all the time," said Azura.

"I know!" said Matt, remembering the swap cards. "But the thing is, he doesn't get caught."

"What if we photograph him stealing something," suggested Paul.

"That won't work," said Azura. "We can't be involved or Klink will just turn it back on us."

They sat in silence for a time before Matt said, "There's a security camera in the food store container."

"Why?" asked Azura.

"Lisa said it's because in the past they've had food stolen."

Azura smiled. "Doesn't worry me if all they steal is meat."

"That's it!" cried Paul, jumping to his feet. "That's what Cameron wants. Meat!"

"Why?"

"To catch a monster eel, of course. He raved on about it during the tramp. He's going to use meat to attract the eel to the surface, then kill it with his pocket knife."

Matt shook his head violently. "No! We're not doing anything to encourage him to catch eels. I don't want him anywhere near Elsa."

"Then we make him believe that Elsa is in some other place," said Azura, smugly. "And I know how."

The boys looked at her, waiting for more.

"Dad carves floating taniwha. He sells heaps of them. They're so good, people think they're real. I could make an eel almost as good. One that would fool everybody if it was far enough out in the water."

"And how does he get out to it?"

"Using one of the kayaks," said Paul. "That'll get him into even more trouble, because he's not allowed to use them. He didn't pass his certificate."

Azura nodded. "Because he can't swim."

Over the next few minutes a plan slowly came together.

Step One: During free time that day, Azura and Paul would make an eel taniwha.

Step Two: Sometime during the day Paul would tell Cam he'd seen a huge eel out in the lake and suggest that he show him the next morning.

Step Three: Azura and Matt would put the taniwha in the lake early Thursday morning before Paul and Cam arrived. Cam would be so excited that he'd steal meat from the freezer. Paul was to mention that would be a good source.

Step Four: When it was known that Cam had stolen the meat, Paul would tell Klink. The security camera would then identify the thief. The resulting search would reveal the orange marker that Paul had hidden in Cam's bag. Cam would confess and Matt would be cleared. Hopefully all this would happen before Cam had a chance to go after Elsa.

Except Matt was not completely convinced by the plan; too many things could go wrong. But the other two were so enthusiastic that in the end he agreed. Anyway, they could stop at any stage if need be. The first three steps were pretty safe. Only the last was one was uncertain.

Matt's first contribution to the plan was to collect some wood for the taniwha. Azura wanted waterlogged wood from the lake, with pieces about the same diameter as Elsa. How these would be used hadn't yet been discussed. All Matt knew was that he had to get them during the kayaking activity that morning.

After breakfast he headed down to the beach with his togs, hoping for the chance to do some swimming after the kayaking. The problem was, Klink was in charge and Matt couldn't be sure what would happen.

Matt soon discovered that his kayaking skills were better than most of the others. The only one anywhere near as good was Maddy. Some of the others didn't even know how to put on a life jacket. When Klink saw how good Matt was, he began using him in the demonstrations and as an instructor. And he kept on using him even after others had passed their certificate and were having free time. Matt was becoming worried there'd be no time left to collect wood.

With three kids left, he took a risk.

"Can Maddy take over from me now?"

"Good idea, Matthew." He then called out to Maddy.

While Maddy was paddling over, Klink turned back to Matt. "Okay. Off you go. You've got seven minutes before you have to report for KP."

Matt went to move off.

"Oh, and Matthew ... thanks for your help this morning. You were great. Keep it up!"

Those were the first words of praise Matt had got from the man. In no way did it make up for all the other stuff, but he did feel a bit more positive about things as he paddled furiously out into the middle of the bay.

In free-kayaking time, they were allowed to go out as far as a small rock poking out of the water between the two bays. The place where he'd seen Elsa on that first day was well within that boundary. Matt went straight there in the hope that she might be around again. With his racing goggles on, he'd be able to see her so much more clearly. He eased out of the kayak and into the water.

She wasn't there, but other fish were; mostly tiny things no bigger than his little finger. Everything was so clear with the sun shining brightly on the surface and no wind to stir up the murk. Seen through his goggles, the trees below looked like creatures with limbs that could trap the unwary. His task was to try and get some of those limbs without getting trapped.

The moment Matt grabbed one of the branches, he knew it wouldn't work: anything thick enough was too strong to break without decent leverage. He returned to the surface to try another approach. Azura had said she'd seen branches close to the shore that would do. Because they would need the taniwha for a only few hours, it didn't matter if they weren't fully preserved like the ones in deeper water. The key thing was that they must be able to float.

Getting back into the kayak from deep water was a skill he hadn't yet achieved. Instead he gave the kayak a decent shove towards the shore and then swam after it. Four goes at that and he was at the edge of the bay, where he found many suitable pieces, even whole trees. Some of them had small twiggy bits attached showing that they hadn't been in the water long. None of these could have been part of the sunken forest. They probably came down the Mokau River when it was in flood. Anyway, some were the perfect size.

Matt loaded the kayak with enough pieces to make several taniwha before pushing it back to the shore.

Klink and Maddy were still working with one student, trying to get him to paddle in a straight line. Matt knew the seven minutes must have been well past, and expected a blast for being late. Instead Klink surprised him with a smile as the waterlogged wood was unloaded.

"You planning to build a sunken raft?" he asked, chuckling.

Matt's eyebrows flicked. "Yeah, something like that."

Carrying the bundle away, he wondered whether a new phase had begun between him and the teacher. If so, then that was welcome, as it would make his chances of getting justice so much easier.

15

MUNN

Matt's second task in the plan for revenge was to find out what meats were in the chiller. As galley slave he was allowed in there, but thought it best if he wasn't seen anywhere near the meat. The only kid they wanted recorded by the security camera was Cam Nelson.

Luckily, each day's menu was on a noticeboard in the cooking area. The meats listed were: ham to make filled rolls for lunch each day, roast chicken for dinner that night, and beef stew on Thursday. This last one was what Cam would be attracted to — lovely chunks of red meat, dripping with blood. Matt would pass that information to Paul, whose job was to convince Cam to go and steal it.

Both Paul and Azura visited Matt during free time before lunch — Azura to find out where he'd put the wood, and Paul asking for fishing line, another material needed to make the taniwha. Matt directed him to the riverbank in the main bay where he'd seen scraps caught on the bushes.

The tramp that day was to Waikareiti, another lake formed by a landslide, this one 18,000 years ago. Matt wouldn't be seeing any of it though as he had KP for the rest of the day.

After the lunch dishes came preparation for a roast dinner that night: 40 pieces each of potato, kumara, parsnip and pumpkin. Altogether a lot of cutting and peeling, which took over an hour.

"What next?" he asked Lisa.

She looked around to see what else needed doing. "Nothing by the looks of it." She turned to Kate. "You got anything?"

Kate shook her head. "Why don't you go off for a while and have some free time, Matt. No use you hanging around here. But be back by quarter to four."

"I don't have a watch."

"You can take mine. We've got plenty of clocks here. That's if you don't mind wearing a lady's watch."

"That one there?" said Matt, pointing to the pink and purple thing on her wrist.

She chuckled. "That's it."

"Okay," he said, knowing there was no one around to see him wearing it. "I'll be back at three forty-five."

Matt took one of the tracks over the ridge to the main bay, a pleasant walk with lots of birds flitting around after insects. Pleasant at the beginning, but not once he reached a brighter area and the smaller insects of the shade were replaced by annoying wasps. So intent was he on avoiding them that he was unaware of someone on the path until a gruff voice spoke.

"Watch it!"

Matt jumped to one side, yelling with surprise.

The voice grunted.

Looking up, Matt got another fright. This was somebody he'd hoped never to see again: the gangster who had attacked him that night back in Gisborne. Instantly, all the fear of that time returned.

Matt moved to take off. Not fast enough. The gangster grabbed his wrist. "Don't run!"

"Leave me alone!" shouted Matt.

Still the man held on. Matt began hacking at the gangster's arm. "Let go! Leave me alone."

"Hey, kid, calm down. I'm not going to hurt you."

But terror had gripped Matt. He had to get away. He started to kick at him.

"All right! All right! Go!"

The moment he was free, Matt took off — and ran smack

into the trunk of a tree.

Collapsing to the ground, he lay stunned for a while. When he recovered, the gangster was towering above.

"You okay?"

Somehow the tone of the voice got through to Matt. This man wasn't threatening; he was trying to help. Now that Matt had calmed a little he was able to see more than the tattooed face and the bulky frame. This wasn't the same man that had attacked him outside Mrs Williams' house. Yes, he was covered with crude tattoos and yes, the way he held his body seemed threatening, but the smile was friendly, even though it revealed several missing teeth.

His arm came out to haul Matt effortlessly to his feet. "Hi, I'm Munn. Sorry I scared you."

Matt nodded his acceptance. "I'm Matt. "

"Mat?" repeated Munn. "Like what you sit on?"

Matt gave a weak smile. "Sort of. Except mine's got two t's. It's short for Matthew. Is Munn short for something?"

The big man looked down at the ground. "Monday is my real name. I haven't used it since I was little."

Matt could understand that.

They stood in embarrassed silence for a time, before Matt said, "Okay Munn, see you around."

Munn flicked his eyebrows. "Yeah. Yeah. See ya."

Matt was about to move off when he noticed Munn moving to pick a frame from off the side of the path. Alarms began to ring in his head.

"Is that a fishing trap?"

"Yeah." Munn held it so that Matt could see it better. "What do you think?"

The trap was roughly constructed from wire and bits of netting. There were lots of gaps. Matt's fears dropped a little. "I made it from an old lampshade."

"Are you after eels?"

"Nah. Koura. You know, freshwater crays."

Matt nodded. He used to catch them in a stream around Hastings. "What do you use for bait? Meat?"

"Nah. Don't need bait. I'll fill this with fern leaves. The koura come in looking for a good place to hide. All you have to do is pull it out of the water quickly enough and they get trapped."

Matt breathed easier: Elsa was unlikely to be attracted to anything like that. "Have you caught many?"

Munn gave a squeaky laugh. "None yet. This is my first try — I'm off to get some fern leaves now. I'll let you know how it works."

Around in the main bay Matt took the vehicle track leading out to the main road. From the bus, he'd seen a track leading down to the river. He was hoping it would give a way around to the waterfall. There was also a sign he wanted to check out, one featuring a skull and crossbones.

The sign came first.

They'd seen a dead possum on the camp craft activity and Matt now realised that it could have been a poisoned one. Maybe the staff should have warned them about the cyanide, because one of the boys had picked the possum up, carrying it around to scare the girls. Humans might not eat the carcasses like dogs would, but if there was still cyanide around the mouth of the possum it could easily poison somebody.

The track down to the river was further up the road and on the opposite side to the sign. Instead of taking it, Matt continued up to the main road where he could look down into the valley and across to the falls. They were impressive even with the reduced flow of water due to the drought. As he stood there watching, he wondered what it would look like in full flood. Those trees he'd found in the water close to the shore that morning would have come over that fall. Now that would be truly spectacular!

He searched the valley floor hoping to see a track leading to the base of the falls. If there was one, it was hidden amongst a forest of cutty grass. Any path through there would be hazardous. He decided to go back to the track and see what that was like.

The first part had steps cut into the clay, making it easier to clamber down the bank. At the bottom, half covered by cutty-grass leaves, was another sign, this one giving the fishing regulations for the river. Clearly this was another fisherman's access. He found the proof of that at the river's edge where Satch was thigh deep in the water, flicking a line back and forth.

"Catching anything?"

Satch turned. "Yep, have a look in the box."

The fish was about as long as Matt's forearm.

"What is it? Rainbow or brown trout?"

"Brown. That's what you catch on rivers like this."

"Then you're only allowed one more."

Satch laughed. "That's right — and I doubt that will happen."

As the man waded ashore Matt checked Kate's watch. Time was passing quickly. There wouldn't be enough time to get to the waterfall and back.

"Nice watch, Matt, " said Satch with a grin, putting down his rod.

"It belongs to one of the cooks at the camp."

"Well, don't take it off anywhere around this place, or

it will disappear." Matt looked at him, puzzled. "How much time have you got?"

"Half an hour before I need to go back."

"Then let me tell you a story ..."

The story he told was this. In 1957, Satch's father, Graham, came to a summer camp at Mokau Landing. One day, during free time, Graham and a group of mates decided to go swimming in the lake a bit further away from the camp than usual. Graham was about to get into the water when he realised he was still wearing his new watch: a Swiss Pierpont that had been a gift from his parents on his fifteenth birthday just a few weeks before. As he didn't want to test its waterproofing, he took it off and put it on the grass under a tree. That was the last he ever saw of it.

When he got out of the water he forgot about it and didn't come back until the next morning. By then the watch had gone. There was a pile of fresh swan poo near the spot, so Graham thought a swan might have shifted it. He and his mates searched around but nothing was found. Maybe it was stolen, suggested one, but no one in the group had seen anybody around there. The conclusion was that, no matter how improbable it seemed, a swan must have taken it away and dropped it somewhere else. Graham returned home without his watch.

But still the mystery stuck in Graham's mind, and many years later, when Satch was ten, the family returned to Mokau Landing for a holiday. Although the watch was not found, the visit started a family tradition: every summer they returned to Waikaremoana and camped for a week or two. Graham and his wife stopped coming when Satch left home and started working. Satch, however, kept up the tradition whenever he could.

"I've searched and I've thought," he said, "but have no more idea now of what might have happened than Dad had almost sixty years ago." He stared into the water as if by some miracle the watch might appear there. "Mum's dead now, and Dad is ailing. I'd dearly love to solve the mystery before he goes, but it's looking less and less likely."

In the pause that followed Matt could see how affected the man was from telling the story. This clearly meant a lot to him.

"Anyway," said Satch with fake brightness, "that's my story. Now what's yours? Why is this boy here listening to me when I saw all of his mates leave in a bus more than an hour ago?"

Matt checked the watch — fifteen minutes before he had to head back. Time enough to tell this man about his woes.

Once he started, it was easy. Easy enough to tell him everything from Mrs Williams' money jar to the events on the Onepoto Track and the punishment that followed.

Satch was a good listener, not interrupting, and asking questions only during pauses.

When Matt had finished, Satch studied the boy for a time before asking, "And this is all true, is it Matt?"

Matt nodded.

"Then what are you going to do about it?"

"Me and my friends have plans for revenge."

"Revenge — or justice? Do you want to make someone suffer or do you want things to be put right? What is it you really want?"

That was a question Matt hadn't thought about. "Justice, I guess."

"Well, make sure it is just that. Because in my experience, revenge always goes wrong and leads to even more trouble."

By now Matt's time was more than up — he'd have to run to be back by 3.45. He didn't mind. He felt good about things. Not just from telling somebody about his troubles, but also from the time with Satch and Munn. It had been an interesting afternoon — possibly more interesting than the tramp.

16

BURMA TRAIL

At dinner that night, Azura, Paul and Matt sat together bringing each other up to date with the plan's progress. Azura and Paul talked about the taniwha they had built.

"You've gotta see it, Matt," said Paul, excitedly. "It floats in the water, moving just like a monstrous eel. It's awesome."

"What keeps it moving?"

"Any small current can do it. Even a breeze."

"It's because of the balance between the two sorts of wood," explained Azura. "The waterlogged pieces are joined to dry wood so that you get something that barely floats. Any movement of air or water makes it twist and look as if it's swimming."

"Sure does," said Paul. "Azura reckons the Loch Ness

monster is probably just something like this but with bigger pieces of wood."

Azura giggled. "Dad thinks it was probably made by some Scotsman as a joke. Now half the world believes it's real."

"So where's our monster?"

"Hidden in some toetoe in the main bay," said Paul.

"It has to stay dry or it will sink too soon," said Azura. "With the ones Dad makes, he coats the dry wood in varnish so that they don't become waterlogged too. We obviously can't do that, so it'll sink after it's been in the water for a while."

"Will it last long enough to fool Cameron?"

"Should do," said Azura.

"And you can bet it *will* fool him," added Paul. "It looks so real."

"Have you told him yet?"

"No, I didn't get a chance. I'll do it later, after the Burma trail."

According to Klink, the Burma trail activity was designed to develop resilience — the ability to cope with life when things go wrong. Matt felt he could have done with a bit more of that but didn't get the chance to take part; he had to clean three barbecues splattered with chicken fat.

During dinner, Klink had explained the rules. A 300-metre-long rope had been threaded through the forest. When all signs of daylight had gone, the class would be guided to one end of the rope. There, they would be released onto the trail at one-minute intervals in an order set by the staff. Each kid then had to make their way to the end of the trail with only the rope to guide them. No torches were allowed. This instruction was repeated another three times to make sure everyone understood. If a person lost the rope, then they were to stay where they were and wait for the tail-end-Charlie, who was an instructor coming through with a torch.

Matt watched the class leave and returned to the kitchen to attack the barbecues. Half an hour passed before Kate gave him the all clear to join the group. He found Klink and Al in the glow of a solar light not far from camp at the end of the trail. The first two kids had made it through.

Squeals, grunts and sounds of breaking branches came from the trail. Every minute or so a kid would pop out, gasping with relief that they'd made it through. Their names would be ticked off the list and they were released to go to their tents.

Jay came through, followed by a couple of girls. Next was Luke and Cam together. Then there was a long gap before a girl arrived.

"Hold it, Melanie," said Klink, as she moved to leave. "What happened to Maddy and Azura. They're meant to be before you.

"Didn't see them," said Melanie.

Klink grunted and waved her off.

Two boys arrived. They were also questioned about Maddy and Azura. Neither had seen them.

Paul came through. He simply shrugged when asked and moved beside Matt. "What's going on?"

"Don't know. Maddy and Azura were meant to be behind Cameron, but they didn't come through."

"Maybe he did something to them?"

Matt nodded. In a way he hoped that Cam had, because this time Matt couldn't be blamed.

By then they could see the light of a torch moving through the bush, presumably the tail-end-Charlie. Shortly afterwards Ms Edwards appeared.

"Did you see Maddy or Azura?" asked Klink.

"Yes, they're on their way." She then moved closer to whisper something.

After listening and nodding his head, Klink turned and yelled, "Okay everyone. Time to go. C'mon, it's all over. Back to your tents."

They went, leaving the solar light where it stood.

Matt wasn't the only one curious about what had happened, but he was the only one who waited at the edge of camp to see if Azura or Maddy appeared.

Five minutes passed before he heard running footsteps coming down the path. Maddy flashed into view for a moment before disappearing towards the girls' tents. Still no Azura.

She arrived a minute or so later. Matt moved out of the shadows. "What happened?"

As she turned he saw her face was tight with anger. "Cameron Nelson happened. That's what!" she snapped, continuing to move forward.

"What did he do?" asked Matt, trailing behind.

Azura kept walking, shaking her head.

"Tell me!" he cried. "Maybe we can use this."

She spun around. "No. We can never use this."

"Why not?"

"Because ..." She stopped and glared at him. "If I tell you, you must promise not to tell anyone else."

"I won't tell."

Still she glared. "Say the words."

"I promise not to tell anyone else."

"Okay," said Azura. "I'll tell you." She breathed deeply for a time before beginning. "The order before me was Luke, Cameron, and Maddy. I'd hardly gone any distance before I caught up with Maddy. She was very frightened. She said she'd heard wasps buzzing in a nest and thought they were going to sting her."

"That can't be right," said Matt, breaking in. "Wasps aren't active at night. They hate the dark."

"I know that, but she was so terrified she wouldn't listen to me. So I said I'd look after her and from there on we did the trail together. I didn't find it too difficult, but Maddy kept imagining things. If low leaves wiped across her face, she'd whimper. When a twig snapped below her feet, she'd jump as if it was a bomb. She really was frightened. The worst places were where the rope had been lifted up over a branch higher than we could reach. We'd have to let go for a few steps before it came down to our level. She would cling to me so tightly I found it difficult to move. Then, when we were about half-way through the trail, she told me that she needed to go to the toilet for a pee. That's when I got mad with her.

"Didn't you go before we left? I asked. 'No, I forgot,' she said. So then I said she'd have to move off the trail and do it there. 'I can't,' she said. Maddy, I said, getting even madder with her, I'm not going to hold your hand while you have a pee. 'So will you stay here and talk to me so I'm not alone?' she asked. Yes, I said, but don't mess around." Azura paused, looking around to check that no one was listening in.

"She went off. Although it was impossible to see anything, I could tell where she was by the whimpering. Then she fell into a hole and screamed. I asked if she was all right, but before she could answer a torch came on. It was that spotlight thing Cameron keeps blinding people with. It took a while for the beam to find Maddy. By then she was standing with her legs crossed. When the bright light hit her she froze like a possum.

"Then Cameron called out 'Hey, hey, hey. Maddy needs a pee-pee, doesn't she!' I yelled at him to turn the light off.

Of course he didn't and she was becoming more and more agitated. He kept on teasing her ... 'Go on, Maddy. Have your pee-pee. We won't look.'

"I could hear Luke laughing as well. I knew what was going to happen. Maddy was never going to squat with the spotlight on, so I left the rope, hoping to stand in the beam so those animals couldn't see. But Maddy couldn't hold on any longer and it happened before I got there. I guess it would have been worse if she'd been wearing shorts. Even with jeans it was bad. A big, dark, wet patch formed. Cameron and Luke were hooting like crazy. Maddy was crying, and I was yelling at Cameron to turn the light off. He did eventually, leaving us in total blackness.

"Even after Cameron and Luke had moved off, we stayed where we were, keeping quiet so that others moving along the rope wouldn't know we were there. Only when Ms Edwards came along with the torch did we move to meet her. All we said was that Maddy had wet her pants and didn't want anyone to see what had happened. Ms Edwards was good, making sure that Maddy could get away and clean-up without the whole camp knowing."

After telling the story, Azura went off to check that Maddy was all right. Matt walked slowly off to his tent, processing what he'd heard. To start with he couldn't understand why they didn't tell Ms Edwards that Cameron was involved. Then he imagined what he would do if it had been him standing in the spotlight, legs crossed just like

Maddy; he would not want anyone to know. To wet his pants in a situation like that would be so humiliating that he would want to curl up and hide. Although he had reason to hate Maddy, at that moment he felt sympathy for her and the embarrassment she'd suffered.

When he got back to the tent Matt expected to find Cameron skiting about what he had done. Instead he was in the middle of an argument with Paul — not a good time to enter. Matt waited outside, listening.

"You're lying, runt. Eels don't swim on the surface. It was a stick."

"It's not a stick," said Paul with a convincing whine. "If you don't believe me, I'll show you first thing in the morning."

"I'm not getting up early just to see some stupid stick."

"I wouldn't mind having a look," said Jay. "It could be that monstrous one that Matt saw. Maybe old ones behave in strange ways, just like old people. This could be the chance to catch it."

Matt felt like cheering Jay for that — it was almost as if he was in on the plan.

"I'm not ready to catch it yet," mumbled Cameron.

"You'll never be ready, will you?" said Paul. "Because you're scared of it."

Matt held his breath. This was a Paul he'd not heard before.

"I'm not scared of it," snarled Cam. "And when I *do* catch

it I'm going to cut it up and stuff some down your throat."

Paul was unfazed. "Then you'll come and look in the morning?"

"I'll come and look, but not to try and catch it."

"Why not?" asked Jay.

"Because I haven't got any meat yet."

"You can get that from the kitchen," said Paul. "They've got heaps in the freezer. Matt's seen it."

"Yeah? Bet it's locked," said Cam.

"No," said Paul.

There was a pause before Cam said, "Yeah, all right. We'll see."

After that there was silence.

Judging this was not yet the right time to go in, Matt went off to the toilet. When he got back the tent was still quiet — until he walked in.

Cam started into him straight away. "Ah, here's the galley slave. Hey, I met a friend of your father's today."

Matt had not spoken to Cam since being punished for his crime, and he'd intended to keep it that way. But this statement changed that. "What friend?"

"One of his prison buddies. This one's got out ... but your dad's still inside, isn't he?"

Matt turned his back to him, even though he was dying to ask Cam how he knew. Out of the corner of his eye he could see Paul looking wide-eyed. Paul wanted to hear Matt say it wasn't true, and at that moment Matt wished more than anything that he could. But all he could do was revert to being silent. That didn't stop Cam going on, though.

"His name's Munn and he's tough as, man. Got these prison tats all over." He then raised his voice to make sure the whole camp heard. "Hey, Matthew. That's what your dad's going to look like when he gets out of prison. He'll have tats everywhere. There'll be one on his forehead that says 'Loser'. That one will be specially for you."

17

TANIWHA

A full bladder woke Matt during darkness on Thursday morning. Too dark to make his way to the toilet without a torch. He lay in his sleeping bag, fidgeting and hoping for daylight before he had a Maddy-like disaster.

"Matt," whispered a voice close by. "The torch is between us. Take that." It was Paul.

Outside, the darkness was more complete than earlier mornings. No stars were visible, presumably hidden by clouds, and a breeze was rustling leaves – signs that the glorious weather they'd had for weeks might be about to break soon. With a bit of luck the rain would stay away until camp finished on Friday morning.

Matt's task that morning was to meet up with Azura at the main bay well before Paul brought the others around at seven o'clock. Because he had no watch, they'd agreed to meet when the first light showed on the horizon. With the cloud cover, that could be later than usual — maybe too late. Matt decided to get dressed and go around in the darkness.

Shielding the torchlight with his hand he entered the tent to grab his togs and goggles. That's when he saw that two sleeping places were empty: his and Cam's.

"He left just after you did," Paul explained in a whisper. "Gone to steal meat, I hope."

"Yes-s-s," whispered Matt, giving him the thumbs up. "See you later."

With Cam loose about the place he decided to take the track over the ridge where he was less likely to run into him. Explaining what he was doing outside in the dark would have been awkward.

Once again his hand masked the light from the torch, letting only a narrow beam shine onto the path. That single act probably saved him from discovery, for the person he could now see coming the other way was taking no precautions. One glimpse of the light ahead and Matt shot behind a tree trunk, torch off and scarcely breathing.

Watching the approaching light, he figured it couldn't be Cam, as he'd not had enough time to get to the other side and come back. Anyway, Cam would be in the kitchen area of the camp, hopefully being photographed by a security camera. The torch was swaying from side to side, suggesting a large male, somebody like Munn or maybe Satch.

Up close there was enough light reflecting off the surroundings to see that it was Munn, seemingly much bulkier than earlier. Only after he'd gone past did Matt see that the extra bulk was a bag on his back.

For a moment he thought of moving out of hiding to talk to him. But Munn was walking with such determination that he let him go. What Matt wanted to know was whether Munn really had been in prison with his father. He thought that would be an incredible coincidence. It was more likely that Cameron had found out from somebody else and was just winding him up: humiliation was his specialty.

Surprisingly, Azura was waiting when Matt arrived at the river. "I couldn't sleep, thinking about what Cameron did to Maddy. We've got to make him pay for that."

"We will." Matt told her what had happened since he'd last seen her.

"Good, then let's get this monster into the water. Here, give us a hand." She led the way into a clump of toetoe. "Matt, meet Tani-Elsa, the monster that will destroy Cameron Nelson."

The taniwha was much bigger and heavier than he'd anticipated. Altogether the six sections joined by fishing line were longer than his body with arms extended. Probably it was much the same length as Elsa, but definitely fatter in places. Seeing the thing stretched out on the grass, he thought it would be impossible to convince Cameron that this collection of firewood was an eel.

In the water, however, the pieces of wood seemed to come alive. Half submerged, they rolled and swayed in exactly the way you'd expect a relaxing monster to float. He began to see that even extreme doubters would be fooled by this mock-up of a giant eel.

They decided that the best place to release Tani-Elsa was directly off the mouth of the river. This was well away from where he'd seen Elsa in the Sunken Forest, and definitely outside the bounds of where they were allowed to kayak. If Cameron did get to go fishing, he would have to break several camp rules which, when added to the stealing, was sure to get him into deeper trouble.

The sky was brightening when Matt put the goggles on and entered the water to join the monster. Azura had attached a loop of fishing line to the head so that it could trail behind as he swam. After trying to swim normally for a few strokes, he gave that up — he'd just end up swimming in circles. Instead, he gripped Tani-Elsa with two hands, lying on his back and frog-kicking in a lifesaving hold they used in training to strengthen legs. That was easier, although much slower than ordinary swimming.

It took longer than expected to get to the release point. By then the light was good enough to make out features on the shore. Matt looked around for Azura, expecting to see her near where he'd entered. She wasn't there. Not anywhere. Had she deserted him? With growing annoyance, he searched the track leading back to the other bay, expecting to see her returning to camp. Instead he saw four shapes rounding the bend. While he couldn't make out any facial features, the body shapes told him that Paul, Cameron, Jay and Luke were on their way. Problem was, Matt was still out in the water, more obvious than the thing they were coming to see.

Taking a deep breath, he ducked below the surface and swam. Four times he had to surface for air, each time barely rising above the surface. He desperately wanted to know where they were, but poking his head up was a sure way to get spotted. He swam on, heading for the side of the river opposite the camping area.

The spot where he reached the shore was thick with raupo reeds. While this provided good cover, he found it extremely difficult to crawl through without creating tell-tale movement in the high stems. With half his body submerged in the swamp, he raised a head to check what was happening on the other shore.

There was nothing to suggest that any of the four had seen anything. They were intent on scanning the surface of the lake searching for the eel.

Except they were looking in the wrong place: Paul was pointing out to the water beyond the camp bay, not the main bay where Matt had released the taniwha. Cam's body language indicated suspicion. If they didn't find the thing soon, he'd give up the hunt.

Then Paul turned in the right direction and began moving towards the mouth of the river. Matt nodded his understanding: Paul must have spotted him in the water and directed their attention elsewhere. Now they would find Tani-Elsa.

They did, and best of all, Cam saw her first. "Yeah!" he yelled. "There's the beast." All signs of suspicion instantly gone.

Soon he and Luke were grunting and hooting. Paul watched and listened, smiling. Jay, who was standing to one side, didn't join in the celebration. Instead he was concentrating on Tani-Elsa — with concern, not disbelief.

For the next few moments Matt's attention was dragged away from the others by a large spider. There were several webs around and it seemed the owner of them objected to his presence. He or she was crawling up Matt's arm displaying an impressive set of fangs. With a flick of a hand it was off his arm and in the water. But that wasn't the end of it. To his amazement, it began walking on water, this time towards the top of his legs.

That's when he decided to move to another place. On hands and knees again, he crawled out to the edge of the reeds, hoping that water spiders didn't like moving water. The new place stank, as if there was something dead around, but he wasn't too worried: unlike spiders, dead things couldn't bite.

In the meantime the others had moved as close as they could to Tani-Elsa without getting wet.

Paul was speaking. "… going to do it?"

"This arvo," replied Cameron. "During free time."

"Better not let Klink catch you in a kayak," said Jay.

Cameron turned on him. "What's your problem, Jay? First you say you don't want to come out with me, and now you're trying to convince me not to go. Have you turned into a wuss like Matthew? Scared of killing an eel?"

"No! I'm just trying to make sure *you* don't kill yourself. I can't see how you're going to lean out of the kayak and catch a monster like that without falling in."

"Don't have to lean out if I use a fishing line, do I?"

"You've got a fishing line?"

"Yeah, Munn gave me his this morning. You oughta see the size of the hooks on it. They're humungous."

Matt groaned. In their plan they'd figured that even if Elsa was attracted to the meat Cameron would never be able to catch her with his hands. But a piece of meat attached to a hook was a different story. There was every chance that she would take it.

Paul must have recognised the problem for he said, "Where is this line?"

"Hidden where you wusses won't find it."

"But what happened to killing the thing with your bare hands?"

"Still am, moron. I'll haul to the shore and kill it there."

"Can I help?" asked Luke.

"Yeah, Luke. You can help, seeing as none of these other wusses will."

That destroyed any further conversation, and soon they were walking back to camp in two separate groups: Cam with Luke, and Paul with Jay. Matt got the feeling that they had just gained an ally.

When he finally felt the coast was clear, Matt eased back into the river. After a few strokes he sensed that something was swimming nearby. Lowering his head into the water, he saw it was Elsa. This was the first decent view he'd had of her swimming. She looked bigger through the goggles: big, and yet so beautiful, her body oscillating, wave-like, as she moved alongside. For a time she matched his speed as if she'd chosen to come out into the deeper water just to be with him. Then, increasing the rate of oscillation, she pulled away.

Up ahead Matt could see something floating in the water. Maybe that was her target. Lifting his head, he saw it was a dead cygnet, about the size of the live ones he'd seen on the first morning. There was no doubting this was the source of the smell. To Matt the dead swan was a stink; to Elsa it was breakfast.

There were no preliminaries, no swimming around to see if

it was okay to eat, no taster. She simply opened her mouth, sucked in the corpse, and kept on swimming. Not all of it was swallowed on the first gulp, a leg was left dangling. Another chomp and that too was gone, leaving nothing behind except a pool of putrid water in a direct line between Matt and the shore. He took a deep breath and swam on.

18

WASPS

That morning, Matt's lot (Group C) had abseiling, led by Al and Judy, the female territorial. They followed a path from the back of the camp that took them up to the main road where they paused to look at the waterfall. It seemed to Matt there was even less water flowing than the day before and he said so.

"That's likely to change," said Al. "The weather forecast is for heavy rain." Several kids groaned.

Al chuckled. "You should consider yourself lucky to have had three days of cloudless skies. That's a rarity around here, I can tell you."

Matt didn't groan. He liked the idea of seeing the falls when the river was in flood.

They moved further up the road to where a rough track

led into the valley. Soon they were standing at the top of the abseiling slope, forming a line to look down to the bottom of the valley. Matt was as nervous as most of the others. The only ones who weren't were the two instructors.

Al described the slope. "The drop is fifteen metres starting at an angle of sixty degrees and getting steeper towards the end. A good beginner's drop. So far, everyone has made it safely to the bottom and I expect that will continue today. There is really nothing to be afraid of. Basically, you'll be walking backwards down a slope. The rope helps you control the speed and stops you from falling if you let go. So let's do it."

He started by attaching the gear to Judy. She then showed how to use the rope to control the rate of descent. Halfway down, she stopped and crabbed first to one side and then the other. After that, she dropped rapidly to the ground to show how fast an experienced climber could go. While she made it look easy, she didn't fool Matt — he was still scared.

Some of his apprehension eased after the first two kids had made their way to the bottom. One of those had panicked, letting go of the rope to grab the rock face. Judy, who was holding the bottom end, simply pulled sharply down on the rope and the boy stopped sliding. Then she talked to him so that he got back to controlling the fall himself.

Before too long, the rope carrying the harness and

helmet was being hauled back up for Matt — there was no getting out of it now.

Going over the edge was the hardest bit as he was reluctant to let all his weight dangle on the rope. Once over that, the descent was almost fun. When Judy called up for him to stop and do the sideways crab, he did so, even jumping out from the rock face like a monkey. After that, arriving at the bottom was a disappointment — he wanted to do it all again.

Next was Maddy. If she was still angry after the humiliation inflicted by Cameron, it didn't show. She backed over the edge as confidently as Judy had at the start. Like kayaking, she'd done abseiling before.

She went down so quickly that Judy had to yell at her to stop and do the sideways crab. By then she was no more than a few metres above the bottom.

The movement to the right went fine, in fact better than anyone else had done, including the instructor. Only when she moved to the left did she run into trouble. No one had done the crab this low on the cliff, and therefore the wasp nest hanging from a bush on that side had not been discovered. Chances are it wouldn't have been that day either, if Maddy had not been showing off her skills.

Three bounds and she went from one side of the cliff to the other, landing with one leg brushing against the bush. The nest was one of the hanging-lightshade types, where the wasps rest on the underside brooding their young.

The moment she touched, twenty or so insects took flight. Maddy saw them, screamed and released the rope. Whether she let go by design or accident, it was the right thing to do for instantly she dropped away from the wasps.

But then, Judy did what she was trained to do, she pulled down on the rope to stop Maddy's fall. That allowed the wasps to catch up.

"Get her down," Matt shouted. "Quick! She's allergic to stings."

"Oh no!" said Judy, releasing some of the pressure, allowing Maddy to slide to the bottom.

Matt grabbed and dragged her into the darkness of the nearby forest. "Are you stung?"

"Yes … no … oh, I don't know!" cried Maddy in a panic.

"Do you have an EpiPen?"

"Yes. It's in the first aid kit."

By then Judy had joined them. "Is she all right?"

"She needs her EpiPen," said Matt. "It's in the first-aid kit."

"I'll need to go up top and get it. Pass me the harness and helmet."

Matt released the harness, while Judy worked on the helmet. Maddy was incapable of doing anything. Only with the helmet off did Matt notice movement in her hair.

"Stay still," he said quietly. "There's an insect in your hair."

"A wasp?"

"No," lied Matt. "A blowfly."

When he looked closely there were three wasps struggling to get away. Their abdomens were arching downwards as they worked their tails, searching for something to sting. He grabbed her hair near the skull and held it out so that they were clear of the neck. Now he had to get them out without himself being stung.

He tried flicking one with a fingernail. That stopped the stinging action, so he flicked it again. Two more flicks had the wasp free and flying towards the light beyond the trees.

"Hurry up," cried Maddy. "What's taking so long?"

"There's some beetles as well."

Now that he knew how to get rid of them, it was easy. The second one was soon gone. The third came out of the hair easily, but instead of heading for the light it turned back, going for Matt's head. He waved a hand and for a moment thought it was gone, until a sharp pain on his wrist located the thing with certainty. Twice more the wasp's stinger found its mark before he slapped down with his other hand reducing it to a squashed mess.

"That's no beetle," said Maddy.

Matt brushed the remains onto the ground. "There were three of them. The other two flew away."

She saw the redness spreading on his wrist. "Oh Matt, you've been stung. Will you be all right?"

"Yeah, I've had them before. It'll hurt for a while. Did any get you?"

She shook her head. "I don't know. I can't feel anything."

"Do you usually feel them?"

"Yes. Yes, they're horrible."

"Do you still want to use the EpiPen?"

Her breathing was returning to normal. "Not yet, but I want it with me, and I want to get away from here."

They waited in the darkness until Judy returned with the first-aid kit.

"Are you all right, Maddy?" she asked.

"I think so," said Maddy. "But Matt got stung."

Matt was sorting through the kit looking for the pen. "It's not here."

"It has to be," said Maddy. "I put it there myself."

"You have a look," he said, holding out the kit.

Maddy pointed to the lid. "That's not the right box. That's Group B's."

Judy's hand went to her mouth. "When I went to collect it this morning Group C's had already gone. Murray must have taken it."

"Mr Klineck?"

"Yes. The pen will be with the kayaking group."

"Just as well we don't need it," said Matt.

"That's not the point," said Maddy, sharply. "What if I had been stung? I would have been dead by the time the pen got to me."

"Sorry," said Judy, quietly.

"Sorry?" said Maddy. "Klink certainly will be. When my

mum finds out about this he's going to be in big trouble."
She turned to Matt. "Take me back to camp. Please. It's
dangerous for me to stay here any longer."

"How come you know about EpiPens?" Maddy asked as
they walked back along the track.

Matt explained about his sister Amy.

"Does she carry the pen with her?"

"No, school says it's too dangerous to have her carrying
it around in case some other kid gets it."

"Same here," said Maddy. "It's a pain. I can't do anything
without having a teacher within reach. Like on the tramps, I
always have to go at the back with the teacher."

Matt nodded. Maybe this was an opportunity. "And get
lost because some moron messes with the markers."

She slowed and turned to him. "Did you turn that marker
around?"

"No. Cameron Nelson did, and I have proof."

"Yes, that's what Azura said."

Time to take a chance. "Why did you support him?"

"What do you mean?"

"You said you didn't see the supplejack, and you must
have."

She lowered her head. "I kicked it over the edge."

"If you'd told Klink that, he might have believed us."

"Doubt it. He was after you all the time. He likes to think he can sort people out. He's after you because of the stealing."

"I didn't steal anything."

"That's not what Aunty Sharon says. She says you stole money from her mother."

Now things began to make sense. "You're related to that lot?"

"No. She's not really my aunty, but she's been a friend of Mum's forever." A pause. "She says your father's in prison. Is that true?"

A nod.

"That's tough."

"And you told Cam?"

"Yeah. Sorry for that."

They walked in silence until camp was within sight.

"What are you going to do about Cam?" asked Maddy.

"Get him into trouble with Klink."

"I might be able to help. After what happened this morning, Klink will do whatever I ask."

Matt turned and studied her. Would it be sensible to trust this girl and tell her everything?

No, there was nothing she'd said to make him like her any more than he had at the start. In fact she was beginning to sound like a scheming witch. And yet … maybe giving her some bits of information might prove useful.

"We're tricking him into taking a kayak to go fishing. If

Klink finds out, he'll be in trouble because he hasn't passed his certificate."

Maddy nodded. "Because he can't swim."

"Yeah. And once Cam's in trouble, we're hoping Klink might believe our story."

"You want justice?"

"Yes."

"I don't," said Maddy, scarcely louder than a whisper. "I want revenge."

19

MISSING MEAT

Matt's first task that day as a galley slave was to prepare the vegies for the beef stew while Kate diced the meat. When they were finished, his pile far outweighed Kate's.

"Looks more like a vegetable stew," commented Lisa, who had been mixing the dumplings that would complete the meal. "What happened to all the meat?"

"That's all there was," said Kate. "I thought it was a bit light."

They looked at each other. "Nobody would steal meat, would they?" said Lisa. "What would they do with it?"

"Dunno, but I thought we were short on snack bars too when I made up the tramp packs. Maybe someone has been in there."

"If they have, then the camera will have caught them. I'll take a look at it later."

Matt listened to this conversation with interest, smiling to himself. Before the afternoon was out, Cameron Nelson would be in serious trouble. With any luck, that would come before he had a chance to go out fishing for Elsa. It didn't worry Matt if he wasn't caught with a kayak. Just as long as his pack was searched and the orange marker found. It would be even better if the fishing bit could be avoided.

Once the stew was simmering away on the barbecues, it was time for the final clean-up. One of Matt's tasks was to dig a hole for the organic waste. Not a particularly pleasant job, but one that allowed for plenty of thinking.

That's when he came up with a plan to make sure Elsa would not be caught on a hook even if Cameron did get to go fishing. He would fill her belly with so much food that she wouldn't need to eat for a week. The food would be the fatty ham and beef offcuts that were part of what he should be burying. He collected them in a plastic bag and hid them in a bush to collect later.

Most of the afternoon had passed before the clean-up was finished, releasing Matt from further duties. And yet he was reluctant to leave because Lisa still hadn't checked the camera. He hung around for a time trying to find a way to remind her. In the end he decided that it was probably better if he wasn't there when it happened, and left to go around and feed Elsa.

Matt sat under the tree with his feet almost in the water. Already laid out on the grass was a trail of food leading to the main supply in the plastic bag. He'd also thrown some pieces of fat into the water where they floated — an attractive feast for any carnivore.

Except Elsa wasn't attracted. He'd been there half an hour without even a ripple indicating there was any life in the water. Not that he was too worried. The dead cygnet she'd had that morning was probably enough to keep her going for a day or so. Still, he did want to see her again before camp finished and there wouldn't be too many opportunities left.

These thoughts were interrupted by talking from behind. He turned to see Satch walking from his tent towards the lake, a phone to his ear. Like many people on a phone outdoors, he spoke much too loudly, loud enough for Matt to hear. He seemed to be giving a set of instructions.

Although they'd never discussed what he did for a living, Matt had assumed by his manner that he was some sort of important person. This phone call confirmed that: the instructions were almost orders and given in a way that assumed obedience.

When he'd finished, Matt stood and walked over. Satch was standing, holding the phone, staring out into the lake.

"Is that a satellite phone?" asked Matt.

"Yes," replied Satch without turning around. "You still a galley slave?"

"Just the dishes to do after dinner and I'm finished."

He pointed out to the lake. "That thing out there. Is that your handiwork?" The 'thing' was Tani-Elsa, still floating, although lower in the water than before.

"Azura and Paul made it, I put it in the water."

"It's very clever. For a moment there I thought I was seeing some living creature." He turned to me. "Is that part of your grand plan for justice?" Matt nodded. "And this boy who is bullying you is going to think it's an eel and go after it?" Another nod. "Sounds very dangerous to me, Matt. Have you considered that he might actually catch a real giant eel."

"Yes. I've got a plan to stop that happening."

"I hope you do, Matt. Because not only is it illegal to take native animals from this lake, I consider it an environmental crime to destroy a creature that has survived so long. That eel should be left in peace until its natural time is done. Feed it if you wish, but don't do anything that will get it killed."

Satch's words sucked all the enthusiasm out of Matt. He'd started the afternoon feeling good, anticipating justice before the day was out. Now he returned to sit under the tree, trying to think of something that would avert disaster.

In the end he decided that the plan was still okay, as

long as Cameron didn't go fishing. His face on the security camera was all they needed. The important thing was to make sure that Lisa had checked it. If not he would have to find some way of convincing her, and that had to be soon. It was time to leave the food for Elsa and return to the kitchen.

He'd not gone far when the bus returned from the tramp. The driver tooted the horn and the kids jeered and waved. Except for Paul, who looked at Matt expectantly from the window. This puzzled him for a moment, and then it clicked: there was something he had failed to do, something critical to the success of their plan. Paul was asking if the orange marker had been put into Cameron's pack. By the time Matt realised this, the bus was well past. He began running.

All three were back in the tent when Matt arrived. Cam was already changing into his togs.

"Where are you going?" asked Matt.

Cam paused to sneer at him. "To catch that monster eel. Why else would I be putting on togs?"

"But how are you going to get out there?"

"What does it matter to you, Matthew? Are you a wussy eel lover too, just like Jay?"

Before Matt could answer, Luke ran into the tent. "Klink's coming," he hissed.

Never before had Matt welcomed the sight of Mr Klineck like he did that afternoon. Klink's timing was perfect.

"Right!' said Klink, towering over them. "We're having a bag search. Everyone stand by your pack."

They did just that, except for Luke, whose pack was in his own tent. He stood in the background looking a bit dopey like he always did.

Klink's eyes went around the tent, pausing for a moment on each of the boys before settling on Matt.

"You're first, Matthew. Empty your pack onto the grass please, including all the pockets."

Matt stood for a moment blinking at him, not understanding. Surely Cameron should have been first. "Why me?"

"Because that's what I decided. Now do it."

His stomach sank. What if Cam had put the meat in his pack? That had to be what Klink was expecting to find.

Piece by piece Matt pulled the stuff out of the bag, all the time expecting to find a squelchy bag of meat. He didn't though, and soon his bag was empty, including the side pockets.

"Hold it upside down and shake it," ordered Klink.

Still nothing. Matt started to relax a little.

"Now turn your sleeping bag inside out."

Matt's heart missed a beat. The sleeping bag was just the sort of place Cameron would choose.

The moment he lifted the bag he knew there was something inside. Now his heart was racing. He pulled the zip all the way around until lay it open. A plastic bag containing something red sat in the bottom.

"Pass that over," said Klink.

Matt did. Grabbing the bottom of the bag Klink shook the contents onto the ground.

"Tell me, Matthew ... why would you keep wet togs in your sleeping bag?"

Good question. He certainly hadn't put them there. "Somebody must think it's a joke."

"Yeah, hilarious," said Klink. He turned to Cameron. "Your turn."

Now that the pressure was off, Matt was able to think a little more logically. What was there to worry about? Even if the meat had been found in his pack, it would've been blamed on Cameron because his photo was the one on the camera. Except with Klink it would be wrong to relax too soon.

Cameron's gear revealed nothing. The same with Jay's.

"Okay, Paul," said Klink, "we'd better do yours as well."

For a moment Paul stood as if frozen in place, his hands shaking.

Klink also saw the nervousness. "C'mon, Paul. What have you got in there?"

Although Paul didn't answer, Matt knew it had to be the orange marker he was worrying about. Instantly he saw that this could work to their advantage.

He took a step forward. "It's okay, Paul. I'll help if you want."

"No, you won't!" said Klink, glaring. "He does it by himself."

Paul had just begun pulling things out when a voice came from outside the tent.

"Mr Klineck, there's a gentleman here to see you." It was Lisa.

Klink took a moment to answer: he didn't want to leave the boys without supervision.

"Send him in."

A moment later, Satch walked in. He looked around and began nodding his head slowly.

"Mr Klineck? Lewis Armstrong. I'm camping around in the other bay." They shook hands. "I think I might have the answer to what you're looking for here." He held up a pink and purple phone. "Is this it?"

Klink turned to Luke. "Run and get Melanie. We need her, pronto." Back to Satch, he asked, "Where did you find it?"

"Another camper found it on a log down by your beach. He didn't have the confidence to hand it in himself, and I was coming around anyway on another matter."

Klink's eyebrows rose. "Which is?"

"There's a heavy rain warning out for this area overnight. Possibly a hundred millimetres of rain in eight hours. You might need to take some precautions."

"Mmm, that much? I could see there was going to be rain but I was hoping it'd hold off until we'd left."

Melanie came in.

"Is this yours?" asked Klink, holding up the phone.

"Yes! Who had it?" said Melanie, aggressively.

"Possibly nobody. Have you had this down by the beach?"

She hesitated. "Yeah ... yesterday during free time."

"And you put it on a log while you went in for a swim?"

Her body slumped. "Yes," she said quietly.

"I think you owe me and these boys an apology."

"Sorry."

"And you need to thank Mr Armstrong here for returning it."

She did.

"Okay, boys, you can pack everything away now." He left.

Before Satch followed, he gave Matt a knowing nod: the man knew that Matt had been accused of stealing again.

"You know him?" asked Cam.

"Yeah, I've talked to him."

"Bet your dad knows him too."

Matt turned away grunting in disgust. What was he on about now?

"You know he's a policeman, don't you?"

Matt's head snapped back. "How do you know that?"

"Munn told me. Says he's one of the big chiefs. District something or other."

"You need to watch out then," Matt said, seizing an opportunity. "He says it's illegal to catch eels in this lake."

"Yeah, so what? He told Munn he couldn't catch koura, but he's still doing it and nothing's happened."

"Are we going then?" asked Luke.

"Yep, right now."

"What are you using for bait?" asked Paul.

Cam sneered at him. "You want to know whether I stole meat from the kitchen, don't you? Well, I didn't. You were trying to get me into trouble, weren't you? Get my picture taken by that security camera. Well, I'm not that stupid, am I?"

"So, what are you using?" asked Jay.

"Possum," said Cameron with a big grin. "I found me a dead possum during camp craft this morning."

"But it'll be poisoned," Matt said, unable to control his dismay.

Cameron shrugged. "So what? *I'm* not going to eat it, the eel is. And it's going to die anyway." He gathered a few things from his pile of belongings. "C'mon Luke. Let's go." Once outside the tent he stopped and poked his head back in. "Hey, wusses, better check your sleeping bags tonight. Because you're likely to find bits of slimy eel in them." He let out a burst of forced laughter, which Matt could still hear long after he was gone.

20

RAIN

There were no bits of eel in Matt's sleeping bag that night.

This was not because Cam had forgotten, but because he never got the chance to catch an eel. He never even made it to the kayaks before the bell began ringing for them to report immediately to the eating area. He and Luke arrived while the staff were doing a head count. The only person after them was Maddy, who, Matt noticed, came from the same direction. He wondered what schemes of revenge she had on her mind.

Klink soon outlined the reason for the meeting: they were to dig trenches around the tents so that they would not get flooded during the night. Everyone had to help and free time was cancelled.

The only exception was Matt, who was called into the

kitchen to clean out the chiller, now almost empty of food. While Lisa showed him what to do, he asked about the missing meat.

"Oh," she said, "when I checked the invoice I found the butcher had misread the order. He supplied six kilos instead of nine. Must be dyslexic."

Despite the reduced amount of meat in the stew most people seemed to think it was okay. Of course Azura didn't: she wouldn't even eat the vegetables or dumplings, because they had been cooked with the meat. Instead she finished off her supply of vegetarian snacks.

As they ate, Azura, Paul and Matt talked about the day's developments. They agreed it had been close to a disaster. Elsa could easily have been poisoned without changing anything: Matt would still have been blamed for switching the signs on the track. Satch was right about the plan being too dangerous. They decided to abandon everything. Seeking justice was less important than keeping Elsa alive.

Ironically, the last episode of *Kidnapped* read that night was all about justice. The plan that Alan Breck and David Balfour designed worked perfectly. Davie got recognised as the heir to the Balfour fortune, along with a good income, until his Uncle Ebenezer died. At that time, Davie would take control of it all. A happy ending for the good guys. Proof that stories didn't always reflect real life: David Balfour got everything, whereas Matthew Smith got nothing.

The rain came soon after lights-out. In a way Matt was pleased, as he found the sound of rain comforting when snuggled down in bed. Although the noise of drops on the tent was different to the iron roof at home, the effect was the same and soon he was asleep.

Three times he woke during the night. The first couple of times, he noted that the rain was still pelting down, before he rolled over and went back to sleep. The third time his bladder was full, and if nothing was done about it there'd be water inside as well as out. Fortunately Paul was always prepared for everything: he must have been the only kid ever to take an umbrella to summer camp. Before they'd gone to sleep, he'd put the umbrella and the torch between the beds so that either he or Matt could use them if need be. Matt certainly had the need.

Outside, the rain was still as heavy as ever. The camping ground was covered in puddles joined by small streams. Matt sprinted across to the portable toilets. They were almost as wet inside as out, plus they stank after four days without being emptied. They were so stinky that afterwards he ran across to the male ablutions block to wash.

The first indication that someone else might be there was a glow of light coming from the entranceway.

"Who's there?" he called, before entering.

No answer. Just a scuffle of movement.

"Who is it?"

This time the light went off. *Strange,* he thought. *Why doesn't he answer?*

He found out why when he took the plunge and entered. The person was not a he, it was a she — Maddy McDonald. She was crouched under a sink, half-covered by a rain jacket, trying to look invisible. It would have worked if Matt hadn't had Paul's torch. As it was, it looked so stupid that he laughed.

"What *are* you doing?"

She sighed and climbed out from her hiding place. "I couldn't sleep."

"So you thought you'd have a wash in the boys' ablutions. Makes sense — not!"

Another sigh. "I was trying to find some way of getting revenge on Cameron."

"How?"

She held up a bottle. "With this."

"Which is?" he asked, puzzled. "Acid, perhaps? Cyanide?"

"No." She sounded disappointed. "I would have used those if I had some. This is just cheap perfume, but it's very strong. I was going to put it in the hand-wash so that he stinks after using it."

Matt stared at her. "But so will everyone else."

"Yeah. That's the problem."

"Won't work on Cameron anyway," he said. "He never washes."

That was it. She left, Matt washed his hands, and they went separate ways. Except, when he got back to his sleeping bag, he found she'd passed on the insomnia. He lay there with eyes open, feeling no drowsiness whatsoever.

Over the next few hours Matt's thoughts ranged everywhere. They started with concern about Maddy and her desire for revenge. Her response about using acid or cyanide had not been a joke. Matt could understand her wanting him to be humiliated, but trying to *hurt* Cam was worrying. She clearly wasn't thinking clearly. Even the perfume idea would've been a problem. The boys would have wanted to know who, and then why — the one thing Maddy didn't want them to know. If she needed revenge, she should aim directly at the target.

Which was advice he should have given himself when seeking justice. The person he needed to work on was Klink, not Cam. If Klink believed Matt shifted the marker, then Matt had to make him believe otherwise.

As he thought about this, he came to a surprising conclusion: he didn't really care anymore. The punishment hadn't been too bad. In fact, he'd enjoyed his time alone in the afternoons, along with the conversations with Satch. He'd swapped two bad friends for two good ones, which was more than he'd expected when camp started. And the encounters with Elsa were something that he was sure to remember for a very long time.

Having come to that conclusion, he now had to make

sure that Cam didn't have one last go at catching a monster eel. The answer, when it came, was to stay close to him. If Cam made any move towards the lake and the kayaks Matt would tell Klink, even if that got him labelled a snitch.

However, as he listened to the continuing rain, he knew he wouldn't even have to do that. The rainy morning would keep Cam in bed until he was forced to get up. It was most unlikely he'd get up early two mornings in a row.

But Matt would. He wanted to see the Mokau Falls after all the rain. This was just the sort of weather that would wash logs down from the bush. Watching them go over the edge would be something worth seeing.

Then, after that, he'd go and see Elsa for one last time and say his farewells until he could return and see her again. Oh yes, he would definitely come back to this place. As far as Matt was concerned, Elsa had turned this camp from disaster into a memorable experience.

And with that thought, he went to sleep.

21

MORNING

The rain had gone when Matt woke. Enough morning light filtered into the wet tent for him to see the shapes. To one side was Jay, his breathing showing he was still asleep. Paul, on the other side, was silent. Cameron more than made up for that, lying on his back, snoring noisily. Matt smiled. Cam wouldn't be going anywhere soon. The worries were over — Elsa would be safe.

Silently, he crawled out of his sleeping bag to get dressed.

Paul stirred. "I'll come too."

Out of the tent, a cool wind was coming off the land, blowing down the inlet out into the middle of the lake. For a moment Matt thought of going back in to get a sweatshirt, but didn't want to risk waking Cam.

They took the track at the back of the camp up to the main road to see the waterfall. Everything was wet: bushes leaked water when touched, huge drops fell from leaves high in the trees, and the ground turned to mud wherever they stepped.

When they finally made it to the viewing spot, the waterfall was a great disappointment. Instead of a raging torrent, there was even less water than before. Only a trickle managed to make it over the edge and dribble down the rocks to the river.

"That's strange," said Paul. "Where's all the water gone?"

Matt was thinking the same. Then the answer came. "Landslide," he said. "Has to be. A slip must have cut it off upstream."

"Yeah!" said Paul. "And there'll be a new lake up there."

"Lake Mokau?"

Paul shook his head. "Nah. I mentioned it first, so I get to name it. Lake Paul sounds good to me."

"How about Lake Elsa?"

"She'd never get up there to see it."

"We could take her up there."

"Or shift some elvers like the Maoris used to do."

For some time they stood staring over the valley, talking nonsense, disappointed that the waterfall had gone, and yet excited that another landslide dam had probably formed. At no stage did they consider that the lake behind it might not last for long …

Back at the main camping area, the boys found Azura standing under the tree looking at the food scraps on the ground.

"Did you put these here?"

"Yeah, but none have gone." The only ones missing were those that Matt had left floating on the water, and the ducks could've got those. He picked up some bits of fat and threw them into the lake, hoping they might still rouse Elsa if she was around.

While waiting, they told Azura about the waterfall.

"Wow!" she said when they'd finished. "So there's another lake around here now, you reckon. I wonder how big that one will be?"

Matt had started to say that he didn't think it would be huge, when another voice broke in.

"What's this about another lake?" Once again Satch had moved up without being detected. Maybe all policemen could do that.

"A new lake up above the waterfall," said Paul.

"Well, we think there is," said Matt. "We think the river has been dammed by a landslide, because there's no water coming over the falls."

The change in Satch's expression was the first warning of any danger.

"You'd better show me," he said. "We'll take my truck."

The truck was the four-wheel-drive vehicle parked by his tent. The moment they climbed inside, Matt knew this was no ordinary vehicle.

"Is this a police car?"

Satch turned. "How did you know I was a policeman?"

"That guy with the tats — Munn — he said you were."

"Yes, it's a police car, and maybe it's just as well I've got it here. We might need some of the special features."

As Satch drove towards the road he began pushing buttons on the console. Static came out of some speakers. More button presses and the static got louder.

"Darn. I'll have to use the sat-phone," he said to himself.

The road was in a bad way. While it was too steep for water to settle, the tyre tracks were now deep ruts where water had streamed down from further up the road — deep enough that the bus would have some difficulty getting out later in the morning.

They bumped and lurched to the main road where they could see the falls. The morning light was brighter and now Matt could see a scar on the mountainside left by a landslide. He pointed it out to Satch.

The policeman nodded. "Yes, that's not far up the river at all. We'd better do something about this." He returned to the truck leaving the others to gaze at the waterless falls.

For several minutes they could hear him talking, without being able to make out any words.

"Okay," he said when he returned. "I've been onto GNS, that's the government geological service. The geologist on duty said that dams formed by slips during heavy rain usually have a very short life. Once they fill up and start overflowing, they can give way soon after, creating problems downstream. They're sending a helicopter to evaluate the situation, but in the meantime he suggests we evacuate the campsites and move to higher ground. So that is what we're going to do.

"First thing we need is an early warning system." He scanned the group. "I need one of you to stay in the truck up here. If there is any increase in the water flow over the falls, that person will set off the siren and start blasting the horn. So who will it be?"

Paul's hand shot up. "I'll do it."

Satch chuckled. "All right. Let me park in a better place and I'll show you what to do."

Two minutes later the truck was parked with police lights flashing through the front grill and out the rear window. If any vehicles came along, Paul was to stop them from going down to the camping grounds.

"All right, Paul, I'll send up an adult to relieve you. When he arrives, you're to report back to your camp. Got that?"

After Paul nodded his understanding, Satch, Azura and Matt left.

"Who's the adult you're going to send up," asked Matt.

"Munn."

Matt's mouth gaped. "You're going to trust Munn with a police car?"

"Munn's okay. He's trying to make a new life for himself. I trust him enough to know he'll do the right thing."

When they got to the track over the ridge, Satch stopped.

"Okay, you two need to go see the camp leader ... Mr Klineck, is it?"

Matt nodded.

"Right. You need to tell him what's happening. Tell him we've got a warning system in place but that they shouldn't wait for that. He should—" Satch stopped because both Azura and Matt were shaking their heads. "What's the problem?"

"He won't believe us," said Azura. "He hates us."

Satch's eyebrows rose. "I doubt that somehow." A pause to think. "But perhaps it would be safer if I went and saw him. I need to brief Munn first though. You two head back to camp."

"Can I go and get my jacket?" asked Azura. "It's down by the shore."

"Yes, there's probably enough time. But if you hear the alarm, run. Run as fast as you can to high ground. I don't know what will happen if the dam bursts, but this flat is probably the last place you want to be. Understand?"

They understood.

At the campground, Satch headed off to Munn's van while Matt and Azura went to the tree. They stood staring

189

at the pieces of fat now floating in the middle of the river, swept there by the wind that was chopping up the surface.

"Maybe she's out in the lake," said Azura, several minutes later.

"I hope so," said Matt. "It's probably safer out there."

Again they waited.

"Listen …" said Azura. "What can you hear?"

Matt listened, unsure of what she was on about. He couldn't hear anything and said so.

"That's right," said Azura. "On other mornings the birds in the bush have been noisy, but there's nothing this morning."

"And no ducks or swans on the lake, either," he added. "They're usually everywhere."

Azura shivered. "They know something's going to happen."

"They'll know something is different because the waterfall is silent," said Matt. "They're spooked by that, not because they know what's going to happen."

"Silence can be very frightening," she said, almost in a whisper.

And then, at that moment, they did hear a sound: the noise of the bell from their camp in the other bay. Klink was getting everyone together – Satch had passed on his message.

"We'd better go," said Matt. "Road or track?"

"Road. I don't like the darkness on the track."

The bell had stopped ringing when they moved off the squelchy grass onto the metalled surface. Walking around the point Matt saw that their bay was not as choppy as the next. The second thing he noticed was a bow wave moving across the surface towards the other shore. The source had to be on their side but was hidden by some trees.

A moment later Matt's stomach dropped and his heart lost its rhythm as his body got ready for something terrible to happen.

That's because he'd worked out that it had to be a kayak making the bow wave, and he also knew who would be powering the paddle. Cameron Nelson had woken from his snores, and was now back on his quest to kill a monster.

22

DISASTER

Matt's nana often said that once one thing goes wrong, everything does. That had certainly been Matt's experience in the ten days since he'd helped old Mrs Williams put out her recycling bin. And yet, he'd still woken that morning thinking that maybe the cycle had been broken and that the end of camp might also be the end of his troubles.

Not so. As Cameron Nelson rounded the point and came into view, Matt understood that the worst was still to come. And yet Cam was only doing what a day before they'd hoped he would. In fact he was breaking more rules than just taking a kayak without permission: he also wasn't wearing a lifejacket, one of Klink's absolute no-no's.

When Azura saw him she grabbed Matt's arm, squeezing tightly. "He's after Elsa," she cried.

By then Cam had seen them. He stopped paddling long enough to give a hand signal and sneer before continuing on his way.

"Cam!" yelled Matt. "Didn't you hear the bell? There's an emergency. You've got to go back."

"You go back, wuss, and when you get there, tell Klink I've gone fishing." That was followed by a burst of raucous laughter.

Azura tried logic. "There's been a landslide. A dam has formed above the falls. It could burst at any time."

"Yeah, yeah, yeah," he chanted. "And everything in its path will be destroyed. I'm not that stupid, Azura. You're not going to stop me catching this eel. I'm on a mission."

"A mission that will get you killed."

"Forget it," Matt said to Azura. "Words won't stop him."

She turned on him. "What will?"

Instead of answering Matt began walking back the way they'd come, quick enough to keep up with the kayak. Already he was considering going into the water if he had to.

Although they were within twenty metres or so of Cam, he made a point of ignoring them as they matched his journey around the point and into the lake beyond the mouth of the river. Matt waited until he'd stopped paddling before making one last attempt to change his mind.

"Cam, it's true. Munn is up in the policeman's vehicle, ready to sound the siren when the dam breaks."

That got his attention. He stopped fiddling with something in the bottom of the kayak, and looked up.

"Munn? In a cop's car?"

"Yes!"

His head went slowly from side to side. "You are desperate, aren't you, Matthew." More head shaking. "The only time Munn will be in a cop car is when he's wearing handcuffs." He went back to whatever he was doing.

Soon afterwards his head came up and he began to scatter stuff around in the water.

"No! Cameron, no!" cried Matt.

"What is it?" asked Azura.

"Possum meat. Poisoned possum meat."

A hand went to her mouth. "Oh my gosh, that will ... oh my gosh."

After spreading the meat, Cam threw a fishing line into the water. Then he fed out a decent length of nylon before stretching out and tying it to a bungee across the front of the kayak.

Azura and Matt watched this horrible scene so intently that for a time they missed seeing another kayak round the point. It had almost made the river when the movement caught Matt's attention. At first he thought it must be Luke coming to see his idol slay the monster. Then he saw that the paddler was much too small for Luke.

"Maddy," said Azura. "What's she doing here?"

Matt knew. Her face showed hatred so intense that she

was almost unrecognisable. Now that she was close to her target she upped the paddle power.

"No, Maddy," Matt yelled. "Don't! He can't swim."

She knew that, of course — that was part of the humiliation. Cam might act like a big tough guy when he was the one with a spotlight in a dark forest, but out in deep water he would be weaker than a baby.

She paddled harder, aiming directly at the place where Cameron was sitting. For a moment he appeared bewildered. But just before she hit, the fear came and he screamed, raising his arms in an attempt to lesson the impact.

If the water had not been so choppy, he would have been killed at that point. The bow of Maddy's kayak would have ridden over the side, smashing straight into his head. That it didn't was only due to the chop pushing Maddy's boat lower in the water, allowing the bow to run under the side rather than over.

Her kayak was going so fast that the whole front section ploughed into the water beneath Cam. For a few seconds the two of them were within arm's-length, with the boy struggling to retain his balance, and Maddy trying to tip him over.

Maddy won.

There was no big splash or anything like that. He slowly toppled out, slipping quietly into the water and disappearing below the surface.

Azura gasped. Matt held his breath, waiting, hoping for

something else. Maddy was staring at the water in shock.

Then Cam surfaced, a boat-length away from the kayak. Now there was splashing, with his arms flailing the water, seeking some sort of support. Matt willed him to stop fighting, to just move his feet and arms slowly. But Cameron was in full panic and his body was no longer controlled by rational thought. He went under again.

Maddy recovered, and began separating the two kayaks with her hands. With them apart, she used the paddle to approach where Cameron had last been. That's when he came to the surface once more, one arm still fighting, the other now holding something. He pulled and his kayak responded, creeping towards him. He'd found the fishing line connected to the bungee.

One thing can be said for Maddy: she arrived there wanting to hurt him, but once she had him in the water, she changed. As the kayak crept towards Cam, she back-paddled out of the way, staying there until he got his hands on the front carry-ring and was mostly safe. Then she turned, and began paddling back the way she had come.

She'd gone no more than ten or so metres when the water erupted behind her. At first Matt thought it was just an unusual whirlpool created by the paddle. But instead of dying away, the movement magnified until the surface was boiling with action. Next, a tail sliced through, flapping furiously, before being pulled back below the water.

For a time the action lessened and was hard to see

against the chop, although it seemed to be moving back towards Cameron's kayak.

"Elsa?" asked Azura.

Matt stayed silent, unwilling to say yes, hoping he was wrong. But a moment later there was no doubt. The surface burst open as Elsa flew into the air, her body writhing and coiling, frantically trying to loosen a fishing hook stuck in her side.

Cam shouted as the huge fish seemed to hang in the air above him, before crashing down into the kayak. There she lay, her tail over the side, motionless. Seconds ticked by, enough for Matt to think she had died. Then once again she was alive, easily tipping the kayak sideways and sliding into the water, the fishing line still trailing behind.

During all this, Cam never lessened his grip, his face reflecting the shock and awe that they all felt. The boy who had come to kill the monster was now in danger of being killed himself. If the fishing line twisted around his body then Elsa could easily drag him under. He must have seen the danger for he stretched out an arm trying to reach the knot that held the line to the bungee. But it was too far, and there was no way that he'd willingly take both hands off the carry-ring.

Everyone waited for Elsa to reappear. She didn't, but from the motion of the kayak, she must have been there still. A couple of times Cameron cried out when something touched his body.

"We've got to make Maddy help," said Azura.

It was a good suggestion, except that when Matt looked around, Maddy was paddling furiously away from the scene, as if it was her life that was in danger. Then he heard what her ears must have already detected: a police siren wailing up the valley, interrupted every few seconds by a blast on a horn. Water was once again flowing over the Mokau Falls.

And yet still Matt hesitated. The alarm meant that water had started flowing, not that the dam had burst. There was still time for things to sort themselves out.

Who knows what he would have done if Elsa had not broken the surface once again. This time he could see the blood flowing from her side where she'd been foul-hooked, the hook itself now buried so deeply that only the loop was visible. He knew then that her writhing was as much in pain as it was to release the line. No longer could he stand there and do nothing.

He turned to Azura. "You go," he said, calmly. "I'll do this." And, without waiting for a response, he plunged into the water.

23

FAILURE

At the very moment Matt was diving into the water, Satch was sprinting along the track over the ridge, coming back from raising the alarm at camp.

Earlier, when he'd arrived at the camp, he'd had trouble locating Klink — no one seemed to know where he was. Eventually Al and he arrived, sweating furiously from a run up to the lookout and back. When told about the dam up the Mokau Valley, Klink immediately rang the bell. A roll call soon identified who was missing: Satch could account for Paul, Azura and Matt, but not for Cameron.

To begin with, nobody was too concerned by this as Cam was well known for his late response to any roll call. A few minutes passed while everyone waited. Long enough that when Maddy offered to go look for him, this was okayed.

Everyone else was sent to get dressed for an immediate tramp up to the lookout — a place well above any danger.

Only when Melanie reported seeing Maddy paddling a kayak out of the bay, did Klink and Satch become suspicious. Then the blasting horn was heard from up the hill. Although the sound of the siren didn't carry, the horn was enough to warn Satch that water was coming over or through the dam. He knew that the greatest threat was in the main bay where there was now likely to be five kids, one of whom had not been told of the danger. That's when he started running, taking the quickest possible route over the ridge.

During the swim out to Cam, Matt saw no sign of Elsa, neither under the water nor above. He hoped that meant she'd somehow dislodged the hook and was free, but feared it meant she was dying.

Cam was in a state of shock when Matt got to him. His hands were white from holding the ring too tightly, his body shaking, his eyes dull with fear.

"Relax," said Matt, touching his arm in reassurance. "The kayak can easily hold you. You'll float better if your body's limp."

Cam looked at him saying nothing.

"We've got to cut the line," said Matt. "Where's your knife?"

Still nothing.

Matt left him then, and, keeping to the side away from the line, moved to the cockpit, hoping the knife was there — it wasn't. Most likely it had tipped over the side either during Maddy's attack or when Elsa had crash-landed. The only hope was to try and release the line by hand.

He took a breath and ducked under the kayak to get to the other side. And there, a couple of metres below, was Elsa. She was still writhing and straining against the taut line, but with less energy than before. Her body was now covered with a milky slime. Was that because of the hook, or was it something else ... perhaps the effect of cyanide poisoning?

Rising on the other side, Matt took hold of the fishing line, expecting to feel her movement. Instead, he found the line was slack. Pulling it tight he discovered that it led in a direction away from the kayak. Releasing the knot on the bungee would not ease Elsa's plight because something else was holding her down.

Diving again, he traced the slack line into the darker water, into the sunken forest. In that light it was difficult to see the nylon clearly, but he saw enough to know that the line was hopelessly tangled around the skeleton-like branches. He tugged, but nothing moved. By then he had to go up for air, surfacing not far from Cameron, who turned and stared.

"Is it still there?" he asked.

"Is what still there?"

"The eel."

"Yes. The line's tangled around a tree. She's stuck down there."

"Good," he said. "Then she'll die."

Matt held his anger in check. Arguing would not help Elsa.

"Do you have the pocketknife?"

"Why? What are you going to do?"

"Release her. Where's the knife?"

"It fell in the water."

Just as Matt had thought. If he was to free her it would have to be without a tool.

This time he dived down past Elsa to the line directly below the hook. The moment he touched it, her movement intensified. As gently as he could, he traced the line to the nearest branch. A few seconds were wasted in a vain attempt to pull it free. That was never going to work. The only way was to use his teeth.

This was not easy with the line so tight and moving wildly. However he did manage to gnaw with his front teeth for a few seconds. Enough to fray the surface. Given enough time it could be successful, but first Matt needed more air.

As soon as he surfaced he knew something had changed. The horn blasts were closer together — Munn's way of saying the water flow had increased.

"What's that noise?" asked Cam.

"The dam must have broken."

"Is that story true?"

Matt didn't bother with a reply. Instead he looked up the river; nothing seemed to have changed there. But things were happening on the shore. Satch was running over the grass heading for the lake, and sprinting towards him were Paul and Azura.

"Go!" yelled Satch waving his arms frantically. "Get to higher ground. Right now!"

Azura stopped and pointed in Matt's direction.

"I'll get them," said Satch. "You go."

She started running again and had passed him when Satch must have taken his eyes off the grass for a moment. His foot hit something that caused his leg to collapse as if turned to jelly. He sprawled to the ground, screaming.

Azura and Paul stopped and turned to look. Satch lifted himself onto his arms and tried to stand, before collapsing back down. As they moved to help, the warning signal changed yet again. This time the horn was blasting continuously — the dam had burst.

Munn's view at that exact moment was later shared with millions of people on YouTube.

As Cam had suggested, Munn had been in many cop cars and knew how they worked. After becoming familiar with the controls needed to sound the alarm, he started exploring the other gear. Of special interest was the video camera on the dashboard. This he adjusted until it was pointing at the top of the waterfall. He switched it on at the same time as the siren.

The first sign that the dam was collapsing was when the flow changed from water to mud. Seconds later, the video showed a tumble of trees, rocks and mud rushing down the upper valley towards the road bridge. Some of the trees were held up there for a few frames before the bridge gave way. Then bridge, trees, rocks and mud flew over the edge to disappear into the lower valley, forty metres below.

Next came the water. From the footage, geologists later estimated that nearly ten million litres of water flowed over the falls in under a minute. Although on the video the sound of this was masked by the siren and blasting horn, you could hear Munn screaming at the wonder of it. Many of his words had to be bleeped out.

What the camera couldn't show was what happened in the valley below where the water landed. A film taken after the disaster showed that the devastation there was total. The water had hit and washed forward to travel many metres up both walls of the valley, before falling back and reforming into one huge blob. It was this that next began the short journey down the river towards the lake.

Matt knew nothing of this when Munn sounded that final alarm. He did shift his focus from Satch to the head of the valley, but noticed no change.

Switching back to the flat, he saw Paul and Azura raising Satch to his feet. They clearly wanted to take him to higher ground, but the policeman had other ideas. A discussion was taking place. The kids must have won, for eventually he allowed them to drag him towards the road. In the last view Matt had of them, Satch had turned his head to give the two boys one final desperate stare.

From then on, Matt's attention was taken with other matters. The view up the valley had changed. Although he still couldn't see any water, the tops of the higher trees were waving from side to side, while the smaller ones were toppling over as if some huge roller was coming down the valley. It was an amazing sight. Even knowing what it must be could not stop him watching, his mind hypnotised by the action. Only when the wall of water burst through did he snap out of it and turn to Cam.

Cam's eyes were wide, locked on the advancing wave.

Matt put his arms around him. "Let go of the kayak. I've got you."

If anything Cam's grip tightened.

"Let go, Cam. The kayak is tied to the bottom. Let go! We've got to float free."

The surge was now coming across the campground. There was no time for anything further. Matt could either let go and try to save himself or stay with Cam and hope that the nylon line snapped allowing the kayak to remain on the surface.

He gripped tighter and waited.

24

LOST

Wherever Munn got that fishing line from, it sure was tough-as. That nylon would not snap, no matter what.

A fraction of a second after the wall hit, Cam and Matt were under the water, the kayak held down by the line, and them by Cam's vice-like grip on the ring. The worst of it was the water rushing past carrying all sorts of rubbish that whipped at their bodies. At one stage Matt thought he saw Elsa alongside, but it could have been just some toetoe flowers. There were plenty of those, and also their cutty-grass leaves, slicing at clothes and bodies.

Still Cameron hung on. Matt tried some of the release moves he'd learnt at lifesaving, but they were designed to work from the front, not from behind. Fortunately, he'd taken a decent breath before being submerged; whether Cam had, he didn't know. Everything might have ended at that stage, if a bigger piece of rubbish hadn't come by. A broken branch smashed into the kayak, with the thick end whipping around onto Cam's head. Instantly Cam's grip loosened, freeing them from the kayak, allowing them to move with the water.

Free of the kayak, but still being tossed around like clothes in a washing machine. Matt would have tried to swim to the surface, if he'd known which way was up.

How long were they were like that?

Matt had no idea. All he knew was that his lungs were running on empty, which would make it over a minute.

Then the surge must have made it out of the inlet into the main part of the lake, where it could spread over a wider area. One moment they were rushing along under the water, the next they were bobbing on the surface moving slowly out into the centre of the lake.

Finally Matt could take a breath — many of them. And with each breath, he squeezed Cam's chest so that at least some air would enter his lungs as well; that's if they weren't full of water.

Again, Matt did not know how much time passed before he felt a movement from Cam: his chest heaved by itself. Soon afterwards Cam was breathing almost normally. Matt had saved him from the washing machine, now he had to get him to land.

There are several standard ways of hauling a victim to

safety. Because Cameron was still unconscious Matt had to use one of the harder ones. This is where you swim on your back doing frog kicks whilst towing the person who is also on their back, all the time making sure that their head stays above the water. It's fine doing that in training over a length or two, but to keep it up for hundreds of metres was near impossible.

The surge had left them in the middle of one of the arms of the star-shaped lake. The two bays at the end of Mokau inlet seemed a long way off. Closer was a rocky headland — Matt went for that.

Twice he stopped to rest, but that proved almost as exhausting as swimming, for he had to tread water strongly enough to keep both afloat. Cam's body didn't seem to want to float at all. If Matt let it go for even a second, Cam's head would begin disappearing below the surface. The only sign of life was his breathing.

From his lifesaving training, Matt knew that the brain could be damaged if it failed to get oxygen for as little as a minute. Maybe that had happened. Whatever the problem, Cam's lack of life made the task very difficult. How much easier things would have been if Cam had been wearing a life jacket ...

And yet they did get there, touching land on a rocky shore at the end of a peninsula — the Puketukutuku Peninsula. Hauling himself out of the water was hard enough for Matt; dragging Cameron out was gruelling. But once again he got it done. He laid him side down on the flattest part of the rock and then lay behind him, unable to move any further.

Some time later, Matt was roused by the sound of a helicopter. Opening his eyes, he saw it was only a small thing, a two-seater, travelling up the arm of the lake towards them.

For a moment he thought they were going to be rescued. Not so. Instead the helicopter banked and turned into Mokau Inlet. These were the geologists arriving to assess the dam. They would find that they were much, much too late.

Matt watched as they flew up the inlet, then the Mokau Valley. They hovered for a time around where the dam must have been, before turning and eventually dropping down to land, presumably at the camping ground.

He wondered how everyone there was doing. Had Paul and Azura got Satch to higher ground before the wave hit? Also Maddy: what had happened to her?

These thoughts were broken by a movement from Cameron. His body was heaving. A moment later he covered the rock with vomit: lots of water mixed with what had probably once been potato crisps — his breakfast, no doubt.

Matt moved to see Cam's face. Although his eyes were open, there was no reaction.

"Cam. Can you hear me?"

Nothing.

Putting his hand on a shoulder Matt shook it a little. "Cameron?"

There were no outward signs that he was sensing anything.

Even though Cam wasn't seeing, Matt didn't like the idea of him staring at vomit all the time. Using the bottom of his T-shirt, he began cleaning Cam's face. The neck chain got in the way, so Matt took it off and placed it to one side so he could finish the job. But there was still the pile of vomit on the rock: rolling Cam over seemed the best solution.

That's when Matt discovered there was something in a pocket of Cam's shorts. Something hard and metallic. Matt knew what it had to be before he'd got it out. It was Cam's pocketknife, the one he'd said had fallen into the water.

Matt looked at it in his hand, anger rising. If Cam hadn't lied about it, this object would have made all the difference. The line holding the kayak to the bottom could have been cut, and Elsa freed from the sunken forest. Instead ... instead, she'd taken the full force of the surge for much longer than they had. Matt wanted to think she had survived, but knew it was a faint hope. Even if the surge hadn't killed her, the cyanide would have. The most hurtful thing was that he'd been so busy looking after Cam that he'd never got the chance to say goodbye.

Holding the knife in front of Cam's eyes, Matt said, "You lied. I could have saved her. You killed her."

Not a flicker of understanding. Matt's anger went as quickly as it had come. There was no point in being mad with this person lying on the rocks. This person was not the one who had caused Matt so many problems; he was not the Cameron Nelson everyone feared. Maybe he never would be again.

Rescue came four hours later.

Luckily, the sun had come out soon after they'd hit land and the wait wasn't too bad. Matt stripped down to his underpants and laid his clothes on the rock to dry but also as a signal in case the helicopter came back. He washed the chain in the lake and laid it alongside. Scooping water with his hands he washed away most of the vomit, making the rock more comfortable. All this time, there was no indication from Cam that he was aware of his surroundings.

Matt's clothes had mostly dried out by the time they were spotted by the helicopter doing a sweep over the lake. The geologists were looking at the rubbish brought down by the surge and saw Matt waving furiously from the rocks. The pilot brought the helicopter in closer. Through a series of hand signals Matt got the message that help would come from across the lake. He got dressed and settled down to wait.

The rescue vehicle was a large water taxi with two

rescuers: the boatman and a first-aid woman from down at the power station.

After the launch eased up to the rock, nose first, a grappling hook was thrown for Matt to secure in a crevice. Then a ramp was pushed over the bow onto the rock.

While she examined Cam, the boatman questioned Matt about what had happened.

Matt told him.

"So you were blasted with all that rubbish we saw out in the lake?"

"Yep."

"That must've been horrific." The boatman shook his head slowly. "And this guy was unconscious all that time?" he asked, indicating Cam.

Matt nodded.

The woman looked up. "How long did he go without breathing?"

"Something like two minutes, I think."

"Mmm," she said. "That could be the problem." She turned to the boatman. "I need to talk to air ambulance about this. Can you get through to them?"

In response, the boatman led the way up the ramp onto the launch. Minutes passed before they returned.

"Okay, Matt," said the woman. "We're taking you both back to Mokau Landing. That's where the rescue helicopter will land. There's another patient to pick up as well — a guy with a suspected broken ankle."

"Was anyone else injured?"

"A few scratches and bruises, but nothing else requiring hospitalisation. Everyone else seems to have made it to high ground before the water hit."

"Thanks to you, I hear," said the boatman. "They're saying you were the one who first noticed the waterfall was dry."

"And my friend Paul," Matt added.

"Well, you better start getting ready for some publicity. A few people are already calling you a hero. And when they hear what you did out on that lake, they're going to know it's true."

25

AFTERMATH

Matt felt anything but a hero as they slowly motored through the debris in Mokau Inlet. Somewhere underneath all that rubbish was Elsa's body, still foul-hooked and tangled in the sunken forest.

It was too easy to blame Cameron. He'd only responded to the situation Matt had helped create. He would never have been out there with a fishing line if Matt hadn't sought revenge. Yes, by then Matt knew it was revenge, not justice he'd been seeking. Four hours of sitting on a rock, thinking, had helped him to see things more clearly. Disasters can do that.

As they approached the shore, he got the chance to study the damage in both bays. The main one was surprisingly clear of rubbish, having been swept clean by the main body of water. One toilet now leaned sideways; Satch's tent had completely disappeared; Munn's van was partially submerged in the lake.

The school camp bay was a mess. The backwash from the surge had pushed a good bit of the rubbish around the point and up onto the camping area. A couple of tents were still standing, the rest had collapsed but stayed in place. The water had mostly lost its energy as it moved up the beach. The most surprising thing was that nobody seemed to be around in either bay. Surely they couldn't still be taking refuge on higher ground?

The launch had docked with the ramp in place before a group emerged from the shadows of the bush. Azura and Paul were there, along with two adults: Al and Ms Edwards. Matt soon learnt that all the others from school had left. With a lot of shoving they'd managed to get the bus over the rutted track up to the main road. Because the bridge had gone, they'd then had to continue on the road to Rotorua, returning to Gisborne via Opotiki — a journey many hours longer than the way they had come.

The group left behind was to care for Satch until the rescue helicopter arrived, and then they would pack up the camp. The truck to carry the gear would also have to travel the long way round and would not arrive until late in the day.

Cam was still comatose when they carried the stretcher to the shade where Satch was lying under a blanket.

Matt was pleased to see that the man seemed mostly

okay. "You broke your ankle, I hear."

Satch nodded. "But you came through all right?"

"Yes." Matt glanced at Cam. "He didn't though."

"Tell us about it."

So Matt told them. Almost everything. The main bit he missed out was to do with the pocket knife. Somehow it didn't seem right to accuse Cam of lying after what had happened to him. Nor did he in anyway blame Cam for Elsa's death. That was his own fault, although he didn't tell the others that.

When he was finished they were silent for a time, processing what they'd heard. Satch was the first to speak. "So you think the eel is dead?"

"Has to be," said Matt. "That rubbish was going so fast."

"Eels are pretty tough animals."

"Not that tough."

"Mmm. Not a very good plan, was it?"

Matt thought it best to remain silent.

After a pause Satch pointed to Cam lying on the stretcher alongside. "Tell me, Matthew. Is that the sort of 'justice' you were after?"

This time Matt did answer. "No. Nothing like that."

After the rescue helicopter had left with Satch and Cam, the rest began packing up the campsite. Matt got a shock walking into his tent. Not because of the rubbish inside, nor how wet everything was, but because Cam's gear was still there alongside Paul's and his — gear that Cam might never need again.

The first stage was to take everything out and hang it over bushes in the sun. Some of the clothes might dry in the time left before sunset, but he doubted the sleeping bags would.

They had all but two tents packed away by the time the truck arrived. The driver had picked up pizzas in Whakatane — more than enough for one each. Matt tucked into the first food he'd had that day. Even though it was cold, that pizza was the best he'd ever tasted.

Also with the truck was a change of clothes for each of them and dry sleeping bags. Matt was surprised to find that the clothes were his own. Tucked under the top piece was a note:

Kia kaha, Matt.
Love you — Nana

Six words that said everything he needed to know: she was aware of what had happened and was thinking of him.

The two remaining tents were shifted to drier spots: one for the males and one for the females. They then worked at clearing the site of rubbish until the remaining daylight had gone.

At supper time they sat around a table sharing stories

from the day. Of course Maddy's story was one of those. The adults already knew she'd taken a kayak around to the other bay. Azura filled them in with what happened there. Except she made it seem that Cameron ended up in the water after a stupid argument between the two. In a way that was true, but surely Azura knew that Maddy's attack was planned in cold blood, not in the heat of the moment.

Ms Edwards then told of what happened to Maddy when the surge hit. By then the rest of the camp had reached the lookout and had a great view down to the water. Maddy was seen paddling into the bay and was part way back to the beach when the backwash arrived. Any other kid at that camp would have been swamped by that wave, but not Maddy. Somehow she kept the kayak straight and rode that wave into the beach, through the gap in the bushes, onto the camping ground, and between a couple of tents, coming to rest only when the wave petered out on the rising ground at the back of the camp.

"We watched her all the way," said Ms Edwards. "When she stopped, she climbed out of the kayak, and stood punching an arm into the air. She sure had enjoyed that ride."

Matt glanced to Azura who responded with a little nod. They both knew there was another interpretation of Maddy's joy.

Later, when the four males were in the tent getting ready for bed, Matt discovered that his body had not come through the day's experiences undamaged.

"You should take a look at yourself," said Paul, his eyes wide.

Matt looked down. The sides of his belly and chest were now covered with bruises from hits he didn't remember.

"Must have been the rubbish in the water."

"It's worse on your back," said Al. "The skin's been broken."

"The wounds of a hero," said the truck driver.

"Hero or not," said Al, "we'd better get them cleaned up before they get infected."

So his wounds were washed with antiseptic and covered with plasters. Now that he'd been told of the injuries, he did feel a stiffness when climbing into the sleeping bag. For a while he lay awake, thinking of how lucky he'd been: a few scratches and bruises seemed nothing compared to what had happened to Cameron. At least Matt was aware of his injuries. The last he'd seen of Cam, he'd not been aware of anything.

When Matt woke, the tent was empty, with sunlight shining through the opening. He found the others helping load the portable toilets onto the truck. They didn't have to do much other than keep them level while the truck driver worked the crane behind the cab.

"You had a good sleep in," said Al.

"A hero's sleep?" added Ms Edwards.

There was that word again — 'hero'.

Matt shrugged. "What time is it?"

"Ten-thirty," said Al. "The school minibus is arriving to pick us up around midday."

"If you want some breakfast," said Ms Edwards, "there's some pizza for you on one of the barbies."

Although the base of the pizza was burnt, it was hot and tasted all right. Matt was still munching away when a police car drove into camp, followed by Satch's vehicle. Altogether four people climbed out, three police and Munn, who acted like he was one of them.

He tilted his head. "Hi Matt, you got back okay?"

"Yeah. You been caught stealing Satch's truck?"

Munn grinned. "Yeah. Nah, I slept the night in it. They're giving me a ride back to Rotorua. My van's gone for a swim in the lake."

"Are you Matthew Smith?" asked the policeman who seemed to be in charge.

Matt confirmed that he was.

"You did well, lad," said the policeman, nodding. "Your actions will not be forgotten."

After that they moved over to where the others were loading the truck. Seeing there were more than enough people to do the job, Matt decided to go across to have a look at the other bay. He told himself that it was to inspect the damage, even though, deep down, he knew it was the faintest of hopes that was driving him there.

Dropping down off the ridge, he had to climb a wall of debris washed up by the surge. He then understood why the flat area was clean — everything had been swept up into the surrounding trees.

Breaking out of the bush into the sunlight of a glorious Saturday morning, he was surprised by how little the bay had changed. Anyone who hadn't witnessed the event would have found it hard to imagine that a disaster had rushed through just the day before. The grass had soaked up the water and was already looking greener after the months-long drought. Even the toetoe had recovered and were mostly standing upright. Yes, one of the toilets was wonky and some trees were lying on their sides, but the rest seemed to have benefited from the inundation.

The most obvious of the felled trees was the one on the edge of the river close to Elsa's home. There, the water had washed away the bank, scouring out the roots until they could no longer support the trunk and branches. If Elsa had survived, she would need to find a new home.

Giving that tree a wide berth, Matt approached the mouth of the river. Swans and ducks had returned from wherever they'd gone to avoid the catastrophe. Life for them was back to normal, even though they had to negotiate passages through the floating rubbish.

Fish had not fared so well. Lots had been killed and

were now floating on the surface. And yet some must have survived, because he could see that a few corpses were bouncing up and down as if being nibbled from below — nothing big enough to be an eel like Elsa though.

Then Matt saw a body.

Floating just short of the reeds where he had once hidden were the remains of a large creature, the skin grey, almost metallic in the bright sunlight. The length was right, the width was right ... and while he could not see a head nor a tail, he was convinced it was Elsa. What else could it be?

Even though he had tried to prepare himself for this moment, grief struck like a blow. His legs went weak and he fell to his knees with feelings a mix of sorrow and guilt. For at that moment, he knew one thing for certain: Elsa would have still been alive if he had not come to her lake. He was the one who had killed her.

26

WATCH

Matt knelt by that shore for ten, fifteen minutes before his emotions came under control. The events of the previous twenty-four hours had drained him emotionally, and if he hadn't been so exhausted, he might have viewed the scene differently. But as it was, he stood and left the lakeside, convinced that the whole disaster had been his fault.

Halfway back across the flat, his thoughts were broken by a flash of light from the riverside. He stopped and looked and yet saw nothing. Had he imagined it? No. There had been a light. Taking a few steps backwards, he saw it again: a flash strong enough to be blinding, coming from the direction of Elsa's tree, the beam so narrow that his head had to be in one exact spot to see it. If he'd been anywhere else on that camping ground he would not have seen it. But he did, and moved to investigate.

Before reaching the tree, he'd worked out what it was. A metal object was wrapped around one of the roots. The flash was sunlight reflecting off the circular glass surface of a watch. Not just any watch, but the one that Satch's father had lost sixty years before.

Not only did Matt know what it was, he knew how it got there. While Graham and the other boys had been swimming, Elsa had come out of the water, picked up the shiny object and taken it back to her home. She would have been about forty then, still a youngster.

On reaching the tree, he saw that a root had grown through the stainless steel band. Most of the metal was covered with a brown film, although some of this had been scratched off as the surge of rubbish and water rushed by. The film on the glass was thin enough in places to see the hands beneath. Satch's dad need not have worried about his watch being watertight, as it was still dry inside after being submerged for all of sixty years.

Pulling out Cam's pocketknife, Matt set about freeing the watch from the root. This was not easy. The roots stretched out over the river that now flowed where they'd once grown. Also, that particular root had bulged either side of the watch, making it thicker and harder to cut. However, by leaning out and cutting small pieces at a time, he whittled it down until it was thin enough to break. After re-pocketing the knife, he grabbed the root with a hand either side of the watch and twisted. The first attempt failed because he couldn't get enough leverage. To break the root, he would have to lean out further. This time he gave it all his strength.

Too much.

The root broke so easily that he lost his balance, falling over the bank into the shallow water. Apart from a few stabs of pain where bruises were bashed, he was unhurt. Most importantly, the watch had been released and was now in his hand.

He lay studying it, thinking about the strange way in which things worked. That it had been Elsa who had first stolen the watch was strange enough. Add to that the fact that for sixty years a growing root had stopped it from being washed away into the sunken forest where it would have been lost forever. And finally, the perfect alignment of sun, glass and his eyes, which allowed the watch to be found. What's more, it was found by somebody who knew of the owner. Satch would get his father's watch back, and, if remarkable things continued, he'd be able to return it before his dad died.

All this time Matt felt water moving around, disturbing the soft sand. He thought it was just eddies formed by the flow of water further out in the river. But increasingly the currents got more vigorous until he knew there was something swimming nearby.

He sat up, patches of fear mingling with threads of hope. Still the animal would not reveal itself and his eyes could not see through water still muddy from the dam.

However, while he couldn't see down into the water, the creature could see up … and a mouth came out and locked onto the watchband. At first, shock made him grip the watch harder. Shock must have also blinded him, because several seconds passed before he realised that the creature was Elsa.

"Stop it, Elsa!" he cried. "Stop it!"

What happened next showed that she also recognised who he was. If she kept fighting for the watch she would easily win. Instead, she let go and, to Matt's great joy, began swimming on the surface, cruising around his body. She looked well. Sure, there were scrapes that weren't there before, but she seemed to be moving much the same. The poisoned possum clearly hadn't affected her — or maybe she hadn't eaten any.

Then she turned around and began swimming in the opposite direction, revealing her other side. This was not so good: the hook and fishing line were still attached.

"You want me to have a look at that?"

She must have, for she stopped moving enough to allow Matt to lightly grip the line. He let it flow through his fingers until he was holding the loose end. He was certain this was where he had gnawed with his teeth. His actions had helped save her. Now he had to finish the job.

"Let's have a look at that hook."

She obliged. In the struggle to get free of the submerged tree, the hook had been torn through the flesh and was now held in place by the skin. Cutting the skin was one option, but Matt was reluctant to open the wound anymore than needed. The other option was to cut off the barb and unthread the hook. Cam's knife had just the right tool — a small pair of pliers with a cutter.

Swapping the watch for the knife in his pocket, he selected the right tool. He had to hold the hook with one hand and twist the pliers with the other. Surprisingly Elsa lay there and let it happen until the job was done.

"There you are. Now you're free."

At the sound of his voice she swam around until once more her head was in his lap. She showed some interest in the pocket knife, but clearly that was not what she was after. He took out the watch and held it in the air outside her reach.

Yes. That was definitely what she wanted.

He almost gave it to her then. And yet it didn't seem right. To her it was probably just something interesting. To Satch and his father it was much more than that: a lost treasure that could bring great joy at a difficult time in their lives. He chose the humans over the eel.

Except Elsa had other ideas. As he tried to get to his feet, she began bashing him with her body.

"Stop it!"

She didn't. If anything she started hitting harder, the blows bringing more pain to his already damaged body.

Eventually he struggled to his feet and made it to the

shore, expecting her to follow. Instead she began cruising back and forward. Matt watched in distress, not wanting to leave her in this way. Just as he was about to give in and hand over the watch, he remembered something else that was shiny and perhaps just as interesting: Cameron's chain.

The moment he had it out of he pocket, her eyes picked up the reflected light. Now she came out of the water, slithering towards his feet. He leant over, dangling the chain at her level. She grabbed it and turned in one motion, sliding back to the water. Without any hint of a farewell, she began swimming towards the other side of the river where, no doubt, she had built a new home. The last Matt saw of her was a dorsal fin disappearing into the reeds.

"Ungrateful thing!" he yelled, before bursting into laughter; some at her actions, a little at his idiotic behaviour, but mostly from the joy of knowing that her life would go on, hopefully for decades to come.

Matt's eyes scanned a little further along the other bank looking for the carcass he'd thought was Elsa. Yes, it was still there, having rolled a little in the water. Now he could see two legs poking from a body: the remains of a deer that must have been washed down from higher up the valley.

Again he laughed, this time solely at himself. He was still chuckling when the school minibus struggled down the track onto the flat.

The time had come to leave Waikaremoana and go back home.

PART THREE

27

HERO

A reporter was hanging around school when they arrived back late Saturday evening. She let them be greeted by the principal and parents before moving in with her questions. Because there was no parent waiting for Matt, he was the first to be interviewed. She already knew who he was and immediately started in with the hero thing.

Matt responded to her questions with basic answers that provided little she didn't already seem to know. Although he was offhand about his role in the whole thing, that didn't make any difference to her enthusiasm for the hero status. Even back then he was becoming wary about what was happening to the story. He already sensed that being a hero might not be such a great thing.

The answers Matt gave were honest up until the stage

when she asked about a monster eel. Then he sort of lied, feeding her the story he had worked out with Paul and Azura riding in the back of the minibus. Yes, they had seen biggish eels up at the lake, and one was bigger than the others, but they didn't think it was monstrous. And yes, Cameron Nelson was out in the water trying to catch eels when the dam broke. Whether he caught one or not was unknown.

The reason for these half-lies was to protect Elsa. If her presence at Mokau Landing became known, then she would be in danger. The group was sure there were many more morons like Cameron who wanted to show how tough they were by killing other creatures, especially those considered to be monsters. Apart from the three of them, only Satch, Cameron and Maddy had seen Elsa. Matt knew Satch wouldn't mention her; Cameron was in no state to talk about anything; and Maddy would succumb to pressure — there were more than enough things she wouldn't want revealed.

Nana got the full story over dinner that night. Matt held back nothing. There was little point as she would know if he wasn't telling her everything. Anyway, he wanted her to know what had happened, so that she could help him through the doubts about his role in the disaster.

"It seems to me," she said as they sat staring at empty

plates, "that this Cameron was going fishing whether you encouraged him or not. He said as much to the policeman right at the beginning, didn't he?"

Matt nodded.

"Then stop blaming yourself. Disasters are often caused by several rare events converging. That's why they don't happen all that often. Nobody could predict that a dam would burst at the same time Cameron was fishing and when that Maddy girl was seeking revenge. What is important is the way you reacted when things went wrong. It seems to me that, from the moment the dam burst, you did everything right. I'm proud of you."

Later, over the dishes, she asked about Satch.

"This policeman, do you know his real name?"

"Lewis Armstrong. Munn says he's a district something or other."

Nana laughed. "Ahh. Then I can see why he's called Satch. A famous jazz trumpet player named Louis Armstrong was called Satchmo. You don't know what district this Satch worked in, do you?"

"Nah, except the police who picked up his truck came from Rotorua. Why do you want to know?"

"Well, you want to get that watch back to him, don't you?"

"Yes."

"Then we have to find where he lives. But first, we've got to get it cleaned and working again."

Matt turned and stared at her. "You think it will still work?"

"Can't see why not. Those old Swiss watches were made to last. If the water didn't get in then it should be fine." A pause. "There's an old guy in Peel Street who can probably do it. Joshua Beadle. You can take it there after school on Monday."

Matt's family came up from Hastings on Sunday: his mother, two sisters and brother. As he hadn't seen them since Christmas, there was plenty to catch up on. They got a shortened version of the events at the lake; just the hero bits, not the taniwha plan.

Of course, sooner or later the conversation got around to his father, Brayden. He was due out of prison in two weeks' time. Although everyone was looking forward to it, Matt could tell that his mum was worried about what would happen then. There was no job and, while he would be eligible for the benefit, there would be a lot less money coming into the home than before. Without thinking too much about it, Matt suggested he stay with Nana until things got sorted out. His mother's relief was obvious, also Nana's. And when he gave it some thought after they'd left, Matt realised that staying in Gizzy was what he wanted too. At least for a time.

Monday ended up being Matthew-the-Hero Day.

The breakfast programme Nana listened to was full of it, with people ringing in to comment on how brave Matthew Smith was and so on. Then when he arrived at school, everyone wanted to talk to him. He'd gone from having almost no friends to hundreds of wannabes. Mrs Snodgrass was especially excited. Prior to camp she'd had Matt seated down the back where he could be ignored; now she wanted him in pride of place up the front.

Not for long, though.

No sooner had class started than a note arrived asking for Matthew Smith to take his bag and report to Mr Klineck's class. To Matt's surprise, he also got the hero treatment there. Klink explained that as things had gone so well at camp, he had arranged for Matt to be promoted to his class for a trial period. Somehow Klink seemed to have forgotten that, before the calamity, he'd had Matt on KP for most of the week. Matt didn't remind him. In fact, he was happy to make the change because it meant he could be with his true friends, Azura and Paul. By the end of the day he was well on the way to making a few more.

The only time Klink mentioned Cam was to give the class an update on his condition. Apparently he was beginning to show an interest in his surroundings and had said a few words to his parents. The doctors were hopeful that there would be no long-term damage. Matt was pleased to hear that news.

After school, Matt walked uptown to the watchmaker's on Peel Street. There was no shop, just a faded sign on a door saying:

Joshua Beadle
Watchmaker

The door opened to a set of narrow wooden stairs, which led to a small room containing Joshua Beadle, a workbench, and lots of cabinets with tiny drawers. Everything was ancient, including Mr Beadle. Not a thing in that room had been made during Matt's lifetime.

"Yes?" said Beadle, peering over his jeweller's glasses. "What do you want?"

"Um, can you repair this for me?" Matt asked holding up the watch.

An arm stretched out over the workbench. "Give it here."

Matt waited while Beadle inspected it closely, through his glasses.

"Pierpont Watch Company. Nineteen fifties by the looks of it. Haven't seen one of these for a while. Where did you get it?"

"Out of Lake Waikaremoana."

A single eyebrow was raised. "That explains the film." His hands went to the bench searching for a tool, which he used to scrape at the watchband. "Mmm, looks like it will come off easily enough."

"How much will it cost?"

"We'll get to that, young man. Firstly, I need to know what you've done to it. Have you tried to wind it?"

"No. I just took it off the root of a tree. I've done nothing else."

"Root of a tree, eh? Sounds like a bit of a story here. Tell me."

So Matt told him, starting with Satch's story and then how the watch had been found sixty years later. He made no mention of an eel, suggesting instead that a swan had shifted the watch back in 1957. Beadle chuckled at that.

"Mmm, interesting story." His attention returned to the watch. "Looks like the water has been kept out so far, but the seals are badly perished. They'll need replacing and they don't make them any more. Most of these Swiss watch companies were forced out of business by the Japanese back in the nineteen eighties." More peering at the watch. "I could make the seals from others, I suppose." He looked up. "Leave it with me. If I can do it, I'll have it ready Thursday."

"Um … how much will it cost?"

Instead of answering, Beadle picked up a newspaper from his bench. "Today's," he said. "Just come." He showed

Matt the front page. "That's you, isn't it."

There was no denying it. The full-face photo was almost life-size.

"I haven't finished reading it yet, but it seems to me you did well there, son." A pause. "So, for you, the cost will be nothing. Come back Thursday and I'll definitely have it fixed. What do you think of that?"

Matt thought it was great and said so. He also thought that being a hero did have some advantages.

28

VILLAIN

The hero bubble burst at exactly 8:07 am on Tuesday morning. Matt knew the exact time because he turned to glare at the radio and saw the hand on Nana's clock change over.

A few minutes before that the radio host had said, "We've got a call coming up from Sharon, who has a different take on the hero status of our Matt Smith. We'll have Sharon straight after this break."

Of course, the name Sharon immediately had Matt alarmed. If it was Sharon Williams, then he suspected there would be trouble.

There was. Her first words were, "Matthew Smith is no hero, he's a thief. A thief and a burglar, and I can prove it."

In the silence that followed both on the radio and in the kitchen Matt heard the tick as Nana's clock changed to

8:07. In his mind he also heard the pop as the shining-hero bubble collapsed to the smeary mess of villain.

What followed was little different to the accusations she'd made in Mrs Dingle's office two weeks before. If anything, her argument was more logical, as if she'd written it down especially for the radio interview. Included was the information that Brayden Smith was in prison and that Matthew Smith had been caught stealing at another school. While her proof – the glass jar found on the empty section – was no better than before, her statements were so definite that people would believe them.

The radio host was generally fair and did question her proof. But Matt got the feeling that he was enjoying the development – a fallen hero was even bigger news than a rising one. This would keep the story going for the rest of the week.

Other calls followed as listeners took sides in the debate. Matt didn't listen to any because it was time to go to school and face his classmates – no longer as a hero, but as a villain.

At first, school was little different from the Monday. That was because few of the kids had heard Sharon Williams on the radio. By interval, things had changed – it seemed that everybody knew. From the comments directed at Matt or overheard, he discovered the most damning information was the fact that his father was in prison. Somehow, in lots of kids' minds, that made the son more guilty.

Not everyone accepted the accusations as fact. Azura and Paul were very supportive. More surprisingly, so too were Maddy and Jay. Maddy was angry at her 'Aunty', saying she often got stories wrong and this had to be one of them. Jay's reaction was strange: he kept telling people that Matt didn't do it, without giving any reasons. When Matt asked him if he had any proof, Jay shrugged and said, "No, I just don't think you're a thief."

Klink's comments were both supportive and worrying. After lunch he took time out to discuss the accusations. He asked the class to consider situations where they'd been accused of things, both things they'd done and things they hadn't. It turned out to be a frank discussion where several kids told their stories. He did it so well that Matt sensed the majority had become sympathetic. The discussion was brought to a close when Klink asked all of them to suspend judgement until they had more information.

"Hopefully that will be soon," he said. "I heard at lunchtime that the police are going to investigate the theft. Perhaps that's something that should have happened before the accusations were made."

This was the development that Matt found worrying.

He arrived home from school that afternoon to find Nana angry — the first time he'd ever seen her that way. Her anger was directed at Sharon Williams and the radio station. Most days she listened to talk-back radio as she cleaned the house and did other chores. That day she'd heard her son's name repeated over and over as callers dragged up things that had happened decades before.

"Why do they let people say those things?" she all but yelled. "Most of it was just lies."

"I'm sorry," said Matt.

As soon as he said the word, she stopped ranting to stare at him. "Oh Matt, I'm not blaming you. You've done nothing wrong."

"Yes, I have."

Her eyes went wide. "What? What did you do? Did you steal that money?"

"No! But I did go back to the house that night."

"You went to that house after I'd gone to bed?"

"Yes."

"Why?"

"Because I lied to you. I said I hadn't told anyone else, but in a way I had."

"Tell me about it."

So Matt told about that afternoon when he'd been used to get stolen cards out of school, and how Cam had been interested in anything valuable in the old lady's house.

"So this Cameron is a thief?" she asked.

"Yes. I think he might have stolen the money."

"This is the boy you saved, isn't it? The one who's in hospital?"

A nod.

"Well, we can't use that, can we? It'll only make things worse if we start accusing him when he can't speak to defend himself." A long pause. "I still don't understand why you went back to the house?"

"I wanted to warn her not to leave the money lying around. I stuck a note under her door. Now the police are going to investigate and they'll find that note."

"Why is that a problem? What did it say?"

"You should lock your money away and not leave it out for people to see."

In the silence that followed, the ticking of the clock seemed deafening.

"Oh Matt, " she said. "That's just the sort of note a kid would leave if they'd seen the jar and stolen it."

Matt lowered his head. "I know. I wasn't thinking too clearly when I wrote it."

She sighed. "But the note wasn't mentioned by Sharon, was it? Was it in an envelope?"

"No. Just a scrap I ripped out of a notebook."

"So it could have been picked up and thrown into the rubbish without being read?"

"Yeah, but that's not all. Someone saw me there at the house." Matt went on and told her about the encounter with the gang member, ending with, "Now that my photo's been in the paper, he might tell the police."

"Maybe not," said Nana. "Gang members don't normally walk into police stations by themselves."

Matt wasn't so sure of that; Munn was one who might.

"What gang was it?"

"The Gizzy Pits."

For the first time since Matt had arrived home, Nana Smith smiled. "Then we definitely don't have to worry. Even if he went to the police they wouldn't believe him. The Gizzy Pits are the town joke."

"Seemed pretty scary to me," said Matt.

"Yes," she said, getting back to being serious, "at night they would be. But they're not our greatest worry. That note concerns me, though. If that's still around there's sure to be trouble."

"What are we going to do, Nana?"

Again the clock ticked many times.

"Wait," she said with a loud sigh. "And hope. There's little else we can do."

Waiting is what Matt did. Waiting and thinking, seemingly all night long. Most of it was senseless worrying about what *might* happen. It was only as morning approached that he began to have some constructive thoughts.

If he hadn't stolen the money, then someone else had. The most likely person was Cam, but what if he hadn't? What if he'd told someone else? Bit by bit, images came floating into Matt's memory. One in particular stood out from the others. This was the quick glance Cam had given when he'd been talking about the pocketknife at camp. Cam had said he'd got it from his older brother. Then Jay had accused Cam of stealing it. At the time, Matt had thought there was something strange about the reaction and he now replayed the scene in his mind.

"Nah," Cam had said, "he owed me." The quick, almost guilty, glance over at Matt had followed.

After that, Jay had asked, "Did *he* steal it?"

Now, lying in bed, Matt remembered there was another glance before Cameron answered. "Got given it by the guy he works for."

Jay: "I thought he was still at school."

Cam: "Yeah, he is. One of his subjects is work experience."

That was all, and yet hidden in there was something to do with the money. Matt was certain of it. Turning on the light, he went to the top drawer of the dresser and took out the pocketknife. He vaguely remembered some information printed on the red plastic handle.

Yes, there it was:

Compliments of
George Mayhill Plumbing
Phone 024 0232 228 724

George Mayhill? Matt had never heard of him. But he could picture the purple van parked behind the old lady's house on the Wednesday morning. If he saw that again, he'd recognise it.

The waiting and hoping was over — now was the time to go on the attack.

29

DETECTIVE SMITH

Nana was surprised to see Matt up so early on Wednesday morning. "What's got you up at this hour?"

"Got something I need to do before school."

"Want to tell me?"

"Not yet."

She gave him a look. "Whatever it is, I hope you've thought it through carefully. Some of the other things you've done haven't been all that clever."

"This'll be okay."

An uncertain nod. "Let me know if you need help."

His first stop was at the nearby shops where there was a phone box and a local map. The phone book gave Matt the address of George Mayhill Plumbing, and the map its location — several kilometres away. If only he had a bike, he'd get there easily. As it was, he'd have to run to make it before George left for work.

The quickest route was down the main road. He'd not run far before a car pulled up alongside. The window glided down and a lady leant across. "Where are you heading?"

Recognising her as a friend of Nana's, Matt told her.

"Hop in. I'll give you a lift."

He did not need to be asked twice.

"You're the hero, aren't you?" she said when they were on their way.

"Yeah, so they say. Well, some of them."

"It's not right, the way they're picking on your father. I know Brayden was pretty wild when he was young, but lots of what I hear on the radio is rubbish."

"You knew him?"

"Of him. Most of the town knew about Brayden Smith when he lived here. As I say, he was pretty wild."

By then they were in the right street.

"This will do, thanks," said Matt.

"I hope it all works out for you, Matthew," she said after coming to a stop. "That Sharon Williams is always shooting her mouth off. I do hope you can prove her wrong."

"I hope so, too," said Matt, closing the door. Then, as she drove away he added, "More than you can imagine."

Those hopes rose when Matt reached the plumber's house: the van in the driveway was the one pictured in his mind. He'd thought quite a bit about what he would do next. The simplest thing would be to go in and talk to George Mayhill. But what sort of reception would he get? Being the Williams' plumber he might side with Sharon, and Matt would get nowhere. Instead he decided to wait. If he was right, then someone else should arrive at the house shortly. He moved a few houses down to sit on a brick fence, partially hidden by a bush.

Sure enough, after five or so minutes a bike raced along the road and pulled into the house behind the van. As the rider dismounted Matt got a good look at him and the bike. There was no doubting that this was Cam's brother: he was big, he swaggered, had a similar spiky haircut, and the same disregard for safety equipment – no bike helmet.

The bike itself was also of interest. This was no machine that had been ridden to school for years. This was shiny new. The sort of bike that a large jarful of money might buy.

A warm glow of satisfaction rose in Matt's body. He was right. Wednesday was the older Nelson's work experience day and Wednesday had been the day the jar was taken. It had to be Wednesday, because Cameron didn't know about the jar until late Tuesday. He must've told his brother that night and the jar had been stolen the next day. Sharon had found out about it either late Wednesday or early Thursday before she accused Matt at school. Everything – absolutely everything – had now fallen into place.

This rosy glow lasted all of ten minutes. During that time he watched George and his helper pack some plumbing gear into the van before driving off to the day's work. Then Matt set off for school.

A short distance along the street he saw a copy of Tuesday's paper poking out of a letter box. He pulled it out to see if there was anything about his affairs. There was. Not a lot. Just enough for the rosy glow to be replaced by icy pits of doubt.

Police to investigate hero

Today's accusation against Matthew Smith will be investigated by police.

Senior Constable Kevin Read of Gisborne police said "it is imperative that the truth be discovered quickly. The reputation of several people is at stake here."

The accusations involve theft of money from an elderly woman's house in mid-February. The exact sum was not known, but was thought to be several hundred dollars.

Ms Sharon Williams, the woman's daughter, first alleged the theft on talk-back radio this morning. This was followed by numerous attacks on Facebook and Twitter. Many of the statements were aimed at the boy's father, Brayden Smith, who is currently serving time in prison on multiple reckless-driving charges.

Matthew Smith was declared a hero after he saved the life of a classmate when a dam burst into Lake Waikaremoana last Friday.

Senior Constable Read said he expected to interview those involved on Wednesday. "I want the matter cleared up by Thursday at the latest."

Ms Williams was not available for comment.

First thing Matt did when he arrived at school was look for Jay. He found him down near the caretaker's shed by himself. His face lit up when Matt arrived. "Hi Matt. What's up?"

"Do you know Cameron's brother?"

Jay's expression dimmed. "Sort of. Why?"

"What's his name?"

"Damien. Why? Do you want to meet him?"

Again Matt ducked the question. "How long has he had that new bike?"

"What new bike? He didn't have one last time I saw him."

"When was that?"

"The weekend before we went to camp."

"Well, he's got one now."

Jay slowly nodded his head. "This is about that old lady's money, isn't it?"

"Yes."

"Cameron didn't take it."

"I know that."

"But you think Damien might have."

"Yes."

Matt left then and went to class.

All morning he expected to be called to the office, and yet nothing happened. The police must have been making their enquiries elsewhere. He knew that sooner or later they'd get around to him, and they did, just after lunchtime.

'They' was just one policeman: Senior Constable Kevin Read, the one quoted in the newspaper. He was seated in Mrs Dingle's office when she led Matt in. The policeman did not stand. His face was scarily serious.

"Matthew, I have to tell you that you do not have to answer my questions. You can also leave at any time you wish, and, if you want to have your caregiver present, that can be arranged. Do you understand?"

"Yes."

"Do you want me to call your nana?" asked Mrs Dingle.

"No, it's all right. I can handle this," Matt said with a confidence he didn't feel.

"All right," said the policeman, "you understand this is about the jar of money missing from Mrs Williams' house two weeks ago?"

Matt nodded.

"Did you see it?"

"Yes."

"Did you return to the house and steal it?"

"No."

"Then how do you explain this?" He held up a plastic evidence bag. At first Matt couldn't make out what was inside, but when he did, his body went limp, as if all hope had been sucked out. Here was the missing torch. Even through the plastic, he could see his name written in large purple letters.

"Where did you get that?" he asked.

"From under a bush on Mrs Williams' section."

Matt had dropped it when frightened by the gang member.

Constable Read continued. "That proves you were outside the house at night, and this proves you were inside." Another evidence bag was presented. This time Matt recognised the contents: the slip of paper with the message had not been lost.

The policeman next held up an exercise book. "The handwriting on the paper in that bag is identical to that in this book, which has your name on it." He turned the book so Matt could see it was his writing book from Mrs Snodgrass's class.

Now, Matt decided, was the time to start defending himself. "Yes, I wrote that note. I slipped it under her door, but I did not go inside."

"And why would you do that?"

"I wanted to warn her not to leave the money sitting around because I remembered that she hadn't put it away after I left."

The policeman's eyebrows rose. "A warning, eh? Seems more like gloating to me ... Ha, ha, I've stolen your money because you were silly enough to leave it lying around."

"I did not steal that money. I did not go back into that house." Then a great idea jumped into his head. "Hey, I know! Test that jar for fingerprints — and mine won't be on it."

Constable Read smiled. "We have tested that jar for prints and there were only two. Some from Mrs Williams and some from her daughter. You're right, yours weren't on it. But most of Mrs Williams' prints had been smudged. Someone had handled that jar wearing gloves ... but I think you already knew that."

Matt remained silent. So much for a great idea.

"Matthew, all the evidence points to you. I think it's time for you to tell us what really happened, don't you?"

This was Matt's chance. He took his time, wanting to get it right. "When Mrs Smith saw me after school on the Tuesday, two other boys were with me. Did she tell you that?"

Constable Read nodded.

"One of them was Cameron Nelson. Know who he is?"

Another nod.

"When Cameron found out I'd been in the house he asked me if I'd seen anything valuable. I said no, but he didn't believe me."

Mrs Dingle leaned forward. "You're not saying Cameron Nelson stole the money, are you? That's not good, Matthew, considering the situation."

"No, I'm not saying Cam did it. His brother Damien did."

"What's this brother got to do with it?" the policeman asked.

"He does job experience with a plumber called George Mayhew."

Silence followed. Matt knew then that he'd scored a hit. Time to force it home.

"George Mayhew is the plumber who was at Mrs Williams' house on the Tuesday and Wednesday. On Wednesday he was helped by Damien as part of his work experience. He's doing it again today. I don't know how Damien took the money, but I do know why. He now has a brand new bike, which he didn't have when he worked at that house."

More silence.

Just in case they hadn't got the message yet, Matt summarised: "Damien Nelson knew there was something worth stealing in the house, because Cameron told him. He also had the chance to find the jar and take it across the road to the empty section ..." He paused, letting that sink in, before adding, "and plumbers often wear gloves, don't they?"

30

ASSEMBLY

Thursday arrived and Senior Constable Read still hadn't made contact, and that was worrying. He'd said that the claims about Damien Nelson would be investigated, but Matt could tell he didn't like someone else solving the case for him. The policeman had promised the newspaper it would be cleared by Thursday. That day had come and Matt had heard nothing.

The breakfast show that morning didn't have anything. Maybe they didn't like being wrong either and wouldn't even announce it if Matt was cleared. He left home wishing for news when he got to school.

All morning Matt kept glancing out the window hoping to see the runner with a note calling him to the office. As lunchtime approached, he became desperate; he'd accept any news, good or bad.

Then the runner did come, but not for him. Instead she had a message to be read out to the class.

There will be an assembly straight after lunchtime.

All students must go straight to the hall when the bell rings.

"What's that for?" asked Melanie when the runner had left.

"There was talk that a policeman might visit today," said Klink. "I gather he is."

Out of the corner of his eye, Matt saw a few of the kids glance his way. He was dying to ask Klink who the policeman was, but didn't dare. Instead he waited until the lunch bell rang and went up to him.

"Do you know the name of this policeman?"

"Yes, but I'm not allowed to tell you."

"Senior Constable Read?"

"Matthew, I said I couldn't tell you."

"Why not?"

"Matthew. Go!"

He went and found Paul and Azura.

"What did you find out?" asked Paul.

"That I'm not allowed to know who the policeman is."

"It can't be bad news about you," said Paul. "They wouldn't be so cruel as to tell the whole school."

"It'll be something to do with the disaster," said Azura. "Maybe Satch is coming to talk about it."

Hearing Satch's name reminded Matt of something he'd forgotten had to be done that day. If Satch was the policeman coming to school then it had to be done quickly.

He turned to Paul. "Can I borrow your bike? I've got to go up town. Now!"

Paul looked at his watch. "Yes, but you'll have to be quick."

Joshua Beadle, the watchmaker, was surprised to see Matt. "I'd thought you'd be coming after school."

"Isn't it ready yet?"

"It's ready. I just haven't packaged it."

He stood and began sorting through some drawers. "You've had an up and down week haven't you," he said, returning to the bench with a small box.

"Yes."

"Is it all sorted yet?"

Matt shook his head.

"Well, for what it's worth, I can't imagine you stealing from an old lady. What you're doing with this watch is a wonderful thing. Criminals don't think of things like this." He pushed the box towards Matt. "Open it."

Inside, sitting on a silk base, was the Pierpont watch looking as good as it had when Satch's father got it for his fifteenth birthday.

"Wow! That's fantastic."

Beadle smiled with pleasure at the reaction. "Came up well, didn't it. Hold it to your ear and listen."

The sound was just as amazing as the appearance. Matt could hear all sorts of cogs and gears clicking into place.

"That's the sound of a well-made Swiss watch," said Beadle. "That will last for another sixty years, easily."

Taking the watch from Matt's hands, he laid it back on the silk lining and snapped the box shut. He then gave a little bow as he presented it. "There you are Matthew. You're a good person. If the police don't know that yet, then I'm sure they'll find out at some stage. Hopefully sooner, rather than later."

Matt nodded. He had the watch, and now had to think of a way to get it to Satch.

Even though he raced back to school, the bell had already gone and everyone was sitting in the hall waiting for the principal to arrive. Klink frowned as Matt tried to sneak in quietly and sit at the back. He signalled for him to move forward and sit with the rest of his class.

Mrs Dingle came up the back stairs, and then waited to one side for someone else to appear. Several seconds passed and some kids had started whispering before the other person arrived. Azura was right: it was Satch, his left leg in a moonboot, a stick in his hand. Matt had seen only fisherman Satch before; this was an altogether different person. In full dress uniform he looked impressive – and intimidating.

He followed Mrs Dingle to the front of the stage where he lowered himself into a chair. The principal went to the microphone.

"Good afternoon school."

The school replied in the usual chant: "Good – after – noon – Mrs – Dingle." Matt did not join in.

"We are very fortunate to have an important guest here this afternoon. Some of you will know him from your summer camp. For the rest of you, he is Inspector Lewis Armstrong, Commander of Taupo Police District. Please give Inspector Armstrong a warm Oneroa welcome."

As the applause died down, Mrs Dingle took the microphone off the stand and handed it to Satch.

"Thank you," said Satch. "I'll not stand because this thing on my leg may cause me to topple over, and I might squash a few of you sitting in the front row."

A sprinkling of giggles came from the students.

"I'm here today because of the remarkable events that happened at Lake Waikaremoana last week. Most of you will have seen the media coverage. Basically, heavy rain caused a landslide, which blocked the Mokau River. A dam formed and then burst, spilling a large amount of water over a waterfall, down a valley and into the lake. It could have been a terrible disaster. As it turned out, nobody was killed and those who were injured are recovering." Here he looked down at his leg before continuing.

"That it was not a worse disaster can be put down to some of you students. As a policeman, I've seen many events such as this, and I know that in some cases the effects could have been lessened if those involved had acted differently. In this case, three of your schoolmates acted just as they should have and I'm here to acknowledge that. I'd like Azura Vauss and Paul Chitwell to come forward."

Azura had rightly predicted what the assembly was about, but her pink face as she walked to the stage showed that she had not expected this. Paul was much more composed, walking forward with a big grin.

When they were on the stage, Satch got to his feet. "These medals that I'm presenting are a thank you from the police and the community for your brave actions under difficult circumstances." He then placed a medal around Azura's neck and Paul's. They nodded their thanks and left the stage.

"The third person," began Satch, still balancing at the front of the stage, "is known to you all. Matthew Smith has had a lot said about him this week, some of it deserved, a lot of it not. He's been labelled a hero and a thief. I'm here today to tell you that the second of those is wrong. Matthew Smith did not steal any money, despite accusations. The police now know who took that money and the person will be dealt with under the Police Diversion Scheme. But just to be sure that other people aren't also unjustly accused, I will tell you that the thief is not a student at this school."

These were words that not just Matt was wanting to hear. Mrs Dingle was beaming down at the school.

Satch continued: "I consider a hero to be someone who does the right thing under pressure even though it may threaten their own survival. Without doubt, Matthew Smith is a hero, and I now invite him to come forward and receive his award."

Matt had got a couple of swimming medals before, so he knew the drill. But he soon found this was nothing like previous events. His legs felt like jelly as he climbed the steps to the stage, the watchcase in his pocket weighing him down like a brick.

When Matt was in place, Satch lowered the medal over his head, saying, "Congratulations Matt. You fully deserve this."

As the applause died, Matt put his hand out for the microphone. For a moment Satch looked surprised, before passing it over as he sat down.

Even as Matt turned to face the school he wasn't sure if he could go through with it. "Um …" he began. "Um … I'd like to say something."

The silence that came over the hall made it even more frightening.

"I'd like to … ah … tell you a story. It's about Satch …

um ... Inspector Armstrong's father."

"Matt. You may call me Satch," the policeman said loud enough for everyone to hear. "All my friends do."

Matt nodded and began again. "I want to tell a story about Satch's father." With growing confidence he told about the events in 1957 when the watch was taken by Elsa, except he said a swan pushed it into the water.

After that he described Satch's quest to find the watch. "For sixty years he looked for that watch, firstly with his parents and then as an adult. He never found it, and probably never would have ... but I did."

At this Matt turned to look at the policeman whose eyes were wide, and mouth gaping.

"The day after the dam burst I returned to the campground and found an uprooted tree. Threaded tightly around one of the roots was this." He then pulled out the watchcase, removed the watch and held it up. "Thanks to Mr Joshua Beadle, a watchmaker on Peel Street, the watch has been returned to its original condition. He claims it will be good for another sixty years." Here, Matt paused to put the watch in the case. "As long as it's not dropped back into Lake Waikaremoana, of course."

After the laughter, he once more turned to Satch. "Satch, I give you this watch so that you can return it to your father. I hope it helps him through his illness and that he gets the chance to wear it for some of those next sixty years."

Satch struggled to his feet and accepted the watch.

Then he leant forward and took Matt in a giant hug. While the school clapped and clapped, the hug went on. There was no way that those down on the floor could know what was going through the policeman's mind at that time, but Matt did. For in that half minute of close contact Matthew Smith discovered another thing to add to all the others he'd learnt over the past two weeks: even policemen have to cry, sometimes.

EPILOGUE

Matthew never did return to live with his family in Hastings.

There were many reasons for this. One was that he was unwilling to leave his new friends. Over the weeks following summer camp, the bond between Paul, Azura and Matt developed into a close friendship. Jay Cross was also sometimes part of this group, but not so close; the others would never discuss Elsa when he was about. The rest of the students in the school viewed the group as somewhat strange kids who shared an intriguing secret – something that they themselves would have liked to be part of.

However the main reason for staying in Gisborne was that Matt's family moved away from Hastings. When Brayden Smith got out of prison he was amazed to receive a job offer from a tourist venture in Taupo. Big Lake Motor

Sports offered tourists all sorts of thrills: stock-cars, drag, drift and formula racing, along with burnouts on several different surfaces. In fact they offered all the things that had put Brayden in prison. If he accepted the job, then he could both demonstrate his skills as well as repair crashed vehicles. The offer was dependent on him signing a declaration that he would no longer take part in any illegal form of racing.

Only after Brayden had accepted the job did the family find out that Inspector Lewis Armstrong had been the one who convinced the company to take on an ex-convict. It was Satch's thank you for being able to return a long-lost watch to his very grateful father.

Cameron Nelson mostly recovered from his ordeal in the lake. The only long-lasting effect was a loss of aggression — something that many others thought was a blessing. When he came out of hospital he didn't return to Oneroa Intermediate, preferring to enrol in another school. Matt would see him around town at times, and they'd exchange nods, without ever speaking. After all, what would they talk about that wouldn't cause embarrassment. Matt could have spoken about the chain that Cam once wore around his neck. But perhaps it was better that Cam didn't know: there would be no joy in finding out that an item once thought so important was now treasured by the eel he had failed to kill.

And Elsa? What had happened to her?

Matt had not seen her since the Saturday after the dam burst. However, he did know she was alive and well because Satch was still a regular visitor to Mokau Inlet. Even though Matt's group had kept her details to themselves, stories about a monster eel in Lake Waikaremoana began to appear on social media and other Internet sites. Matt kept track of these stories, but was not worried by them. Without exception the stories were about a humungous killer that should be avoided for fear of your life. Not one of them described a gentle creature that liked sausages and shiny things.

If ever a story did arise about a taniwha wearing a silvery chain, then Matt would start worrying. But for now he would live with the memories of what she was really like. Yes, he would visit her one day, but he'd let it happen in its own way. Because amongst the many things he'd learnt from this experience was that events had a way of sorting themselves out. You never really knew what might happen. Even something as simple as helping an old lady put out the rubbish could lead to things you would never imagine.

COOL NUKES

by Des Hunt

TAKE 1 cutting-edge science professor.
ADD 2 shocking laboratory explosions.
MIX IN an avalanche of cryptic messages and
3 science-geek students …

and you have the recipe for a nuclear
device that could solve all of humankind's
energy problems!

Max, Jian Xin and Cleo are making something
spectacular for the ExpoFest science fair.
If it works, their machine will be worth
a fortune — **but is it worth a life?**

PROJECT HUIA

by Des Hunt

"She fell from the air, her wings no more
use than a ripped parachute."

With a flash of yellow wattles glowing against the sheen
of her black feathers, the frightened huia whirls clumsily
across the rugged gorge. Mavis and Jim scramble after the
injured bird, but to reach her they have to take a jigger
through the long, dark rail tunnel. And, halfway through,
they hear the roar of an approaching train ...

Fighting a family of thugs and a long-lasting jinx, Logan
and Grandpop Jim attempt to unravel the mystery of a
huia that vanished long ago.

ABOUT THE AUTHOR

Des Hunt was a science and technology teacher for many years, interspersed with periods of curriculum development both in New Zealand and overseas. During this time he had several textbooks published to support the New Zealand curriculum. Over the last twenty years he has experimented with other ways of interesting youngsters in science, creating computer games and writing non-fiction and fiction with scientific themes.

After living in Auckland for much of his life he moved with his wife, Lynne, to Matarangi on New Zealand's Coromandel Peninsula. He retired from the classroom in 2007 to concentrate on writing fiction for children. He continues his aim of fostering young peoples' natural interest in the science of their surroundings by visiting schools and libraries, where he runs workshops and presentations.